The Curious Tale

OF

Marmalade Tuttle

By
Bob Trotter

BOOK ONE

Marmalade Tuttle And The Wizard of Caldor

ℰ
Eloquent Books
New York, New York

Copyright © 2008

Eloquent Books or Strategic Book Publishing
An imprint of Writers Literary & Publishing Services, Inc.
845 Third Avenue, 6th Floor – 6016
New York, NY 10022
http://www.strategicbookpublishing.com

ISBN 978-1-60693-014-4   1-60693-014-1

For Hannah and Katie.
Also special thanks to Rachel, my first critic.

Table of Contents

Chapter One

Marmalade Tuttle was a twelve-year-old girl; in fact, she was nearly thirteen. She wore jeans, a striped blue-and-white T-shirt, and trainers, and she had an old red rucksack in which she carried all the things that any girl her age would carry. She had long ginger hair that was always tied in a ponytail, and freckles that she absolutely hated. But, Marmalade Tuttle was different, because Marmalade Tuttle was a witch!

Like any girl her age, though, Marmalade went to school, had lots of friends, listened to music on her MP3 player, had a mobile phone, a Game Boy, and loved looking at all the latest fashions in her magazines. None of her friends knew that she was a witch, and Marmalade was determined to keep it that way.

Anyway, it's not as if she was the sort of witch that flew around on Halloween night on a broomstick, with a pointy hat, cackling and screaming and scaring the lives out of young kids; she wasn't even a very experienced witch, as she was only a level two, but a witch nonetheless. She was the latest in a long line of Tuttle witches that stretched back hundreds of years, and although there were times in her life when she didn't really like being a witch, deep down she was secretly very proud of it. It was even said that her father was a descendant of the Great Merlin himself, but Marmalade took that with a pinch of salt and thought that it was probably more exaggeration than fact.

Marmalade lived in a very large old house, about ten minutes walk from her school with her mother, Imelda, and her aunts

Winifred and Prudence, all of whom were witches and all of whom claimed to be at least 300 years old. Her aunts looked the way maiden aunts should, but her mother was very tall and very slim. She looked to be in her mid thirties, and to Marmalade, she was very beautiful.

Although she loved her house, it tended to act very strangely at times. For instance, the gate and the post-box at the front of the path would speak, but only to witches, and the furniture in the house would move around as the notion took it. One day you could walk into a room that was the kitchen, and the next day it would be a bathroom or a bedroom, depending on what mood the furniture was in. Sometimes it didn't move for days, and then for some reason it would move every day for a week. It was as if it got fed up staying in the one place, and that could make life very confusing.

Even the stairs were decidedly odd. Sometimes they would let you go up and down, and other days they simply refused. So, as you can imagine, Marmalade never had any of her friends round for parties, sleepovers or anything like that. She would always fob them off with some excuse, like her aunts were ill, or the painters were in, or the house was being fumigated — anything that would put her friends off — and it got to the stage that her friends simply gave up asking, or waiting to be asked.

Although her mum and aunts were level twelve witches, the highest level that a witch could reach, they had great difficulty understanding 21st century technology. Sure, they could do spells for this and that, but ask them to use a DVD or a microwave or even send a text message on a mobile phone, and they were completely lost. Marmalade thought her aunts were a bit scatty, especially her Aunt Prudence, who insisted that she could communicate with all living things, and would spend hours in the greenhouse apparently having polite conversation with all manner of plants and insects.

Meanwhile, her Aunt Winifred had been working on a spell for at least eighty years called "The Answer to Everything Spell," but was no further on now than the day she started. But that was all part of the Tuttle household, and Marmalade had grown to accept it as normal.

Chapter Two

One Friday afternoon, Marmalade arrived home as usual at around 3:30 p.m., looking forward to the weekend. She had arranged to meet some of her friends in town the next day for a walk around the shops and a pizza, and then go to the movies.

But as she approached the house, she could hear what sounded like wailing coming from inside. *What's wrong now?* she thought as she opened the gate.

"I wouldn't go in there if I were you," Gate said.

"No, most definitely not," confirmed Post-box.

"Oh, and why not?" Marmalade asked.

"There's something very strange afoot," answered Gate.

"Yes, something very, very strange," echoed Post-box.

"There is ALWAYS something strange afoot," replied Marmalade. "This is a witch's house, and the fact that I am standing here, talking to a gate and a post-box, should tell you that."

"Ah, but this is different," said Gate, smugly.

"Yes, very different," repeated Post-box.

"Why?" asked Marmalade. "What makes THIS so different?"

"Don't know," answered Gate, "it just is."

"Yes," echoed Post-Box again, "we don't know, but it just is."

"You two are intolerable," said Marmalade, walking up the path.

"Well, don't say we didn't warn you," Gate shouted after her.

"Yes, don't say we didn't warn you," repeated Post-box.

"Yes, thank you," called Marmalade as she reached the door and turned her key.

As Marmalade went to let herself in, she had to admit that maybe Gate and Post-Box were right for a change; it did seem very peculiar that she could hear her two aunts obviously very upset about something, and she couldn't hear her mother's voice at all. *Maybe I should ask Biscuit first and see what's happening,* she thought.

Biscuit was Marmalade's ferret. Some witches have cats, some have owls, some even have lizards or frogs, but Marmalade had a ferret. When she walked round to the back of the house, she found Biscuit lying on the grass, with his front paws covering his ears. Marmalade sat down beside him.

"What's all the commotion about?" she asked.

"Search me," replied Biscuit. "It all started after you went to school this morning, and hasn't stopped since. Your aunts have been screeching and running around the house shouting something about being doomed and what to do, what to do. So I came out here."

"Where's Mum?" asked Marmalade, starting to get worried.

"In bed, I think," replied Biscuit. "It seems she's the cause of all this. Something about her losing her powers and finding somebody called Beatticus Twigg."

"What?" gasped Marmalade in horror. "Mum has got MORLOCKINS?" Morlockins was what happened when a witch or wizard lost their powers, and as far as anyone could remember it had only happened a few times in recorded history, and how to recognize it is one of the very first things that a witch is taught.

"Apparently so," replied Biscuit, "and they need to find this Beatticus bloke to cure her."

"Well, did they find him?" asked Marmalade, getting more and more worried.

"Haven't a clue," replied Biscuit. "I stayed well out of the way."

"A great lot of help you are," said Marmalade, getting to her feet. "Come on. We better see what's happening."

Marmalade and Biscuit ran in through the back door, and could hear Winifred and Prudence still running around the house. "Aunt Winifred, Aunt Prudence, what's wrong?" asked Marmalade. Her two aunts ran over and threw their arms around her.

"Marmalade, thank goodness you're home," said Prudence.

"It's terrible, terrible," shrieked Winifred. "Poor Imelda, what are we going to do? It's disastrous, disastrous, I tell you."

"Calm down," said Marmalade, "and tell me what happened."

"Well," explained Prudence, taking a deep breath, "you know how Winifred has been working on this spell thingy of hers? She and your poor mother were down in the basement when it happened."

"When what happened?" asked Marmalade, wishing that her aunts would get to the point.

"The MORLOCKINS!" whispered Winifred. "One second she was perfectly fine, and we were crushing some beetles, and the next, POOF! She stood bolt upright with a very large grin on her face, rigid as a pole, and then she crossed her arms and toppled over, stiff as a board. She has been like that ever since. Poor Imelda, it's entirely my fault."

Marmalade knew that those were the classic signs of Morlockins. "Where is she now?"

"We carried her up to her room and laid her on top of the bed," replied Prudence, "stiff as a poker she is and grinning like a Cheshire cat. We had terrible trouble getting her around the corner at the top of the landing. Didn't we, Winifred?"

"Yes, terrible trouble," Winifred replied.

Marmalade ran upstairs to her mother's room, closely followed by her two aunts and Biscuit. Her mother was lying on the bed staring at the ceiling with a very large grin on her face, her arms folded across her chest, and as her aunts had said, she was completely stiff. Biscuit chuckled, and Marmalade gave him a very cross look. Then she waved and clicked her fingers in front of her mother's face, but there was no reaction, not so much as a blink of an eye. Her aunts began wailing again.

"Wailing isn't going to help," said Marmalade. "We need to think about what we can do."

"There is only one thing we can do," said Prudence.

"Yes, we need to find Beatticus Twigg," added Winifred. "He is the only one who can help her."

"Who is Beatticus Twigg?" asked Marmalade.

"No one really knows who or what he is," replied Winifred in hushed tones. "Some say he was the first Great Wizard, as old as the Witchings itself, and that Merlin was once his apprentice. Some say he is a Druid, a Soothsayer, and an Oracle who can communicate with nature and has the answers to all the questions that have ever been asked since time began, but then others believe that he is just some crazy old hermit who lives in a cave and is as mad as a hatter."

"Well, where do we have to go to find him?" asked Marmalade.

"That's the problem, dear," replied Prudence. "He lives on the, er, OTHER SIDE, through the Portal."

Marmalade stared at her aunts. "Portal, what Portal?"

"The one behind the cooker in the kitchen, dear," replied Winifred.

"There is a Portal behind our cooker in the kitchen?" asked Marmalade in disbelief.

"Why yes, of course there is, dear," answered Prudence, laughing. "Every witch's house has a Portal, to get to The Other Side," she stated very matter-of-factly. "I thought you knew that."

Marmalade sat on the bed beside her mum, trying to take in all that had happened and thinking that it was times like this that she wished she had a normal family. A family without talking gates and post-boxes, without moving furniture, without witches, and certainly without Portals.

Chapter Three

Marmalade stood up and looked at her mum. Although she had Morlockins, she looked very happy. In fact, she had never seen her mum smile so much. "Is she in any pain?" she asked her aunts.

"Dear me, child, no," replied Prudence, "and she is probably aware that we are talking about her, I think. That's the thing about Morlockins. It happens so rarely that nobody really knows much about it."

"So what do we do now?" asked Marmalade.

"Well, someone will have to go through the Portal to The Other Side and find Beatticus," replied Winifred.

"Someone meaning me, I suppose." Marmalade sighed.

"Well, you are the youngest and fittest, dear," replied Winifred, "and you can take Biscuit with you to keep you company. Prudence and I need to stay here and look after your poor mother."

"I'm not going through any Portal," protested Biscuit, looking at Marmalade.

"Oh, yes you are," answered Marmalade firmly. "If I'm going, you're going." Biscuit sighed. "How long does Morlockins last?" she continued.

"Who knows," Prudence replied. "Only Beatticus would have any idea, and only he can cure it."

"And what is on The Other Side?"

"Oh it's a marvelous place," replied Winifred, waving her arms about, "with all sorts of strange and wonderful things. The sun always shines, and it is all so peaceful and quiet. We absolutely adore it."

"I'm not too sure about this," said Marmalade. "I'm only a level two. How would I know how to find this Beatticus?"

"Oh, someone will help you, dear," replied Winifred. "Beatticus can't be that hard to find. After all, it is said that he was the one who created The Other Side."

"Come," said Prudence, "let's leave your mother in peace and go down to the kitchen, get you ready, and open up the Portal."

Marmalade looked down at her mother and sighed. *Bang goes my pizza and movie,* she thought as she kissed her mother on the cheek and closed the bedroom door behind her.

Chapter Four

Marmalade followed her aunts into the kitchen, with Biscuit walking beside her, still not sure if SHE was the right person to go to The Other Side.

"Do I have to go right now?" she asked.

"Of course, dear, the sooner you go, the sooner you can find Beatticus, and the sooner your poor mother can be cured," replied Winifred.

"But what do I take with me?"

"Whatever you like," answered Prudence. "Just remember that whatever you take, you can't bring back, so just take stuff that you won't need to bring back. Food and drinks are okay, and your spell book, but anything other than that, I'm afraid you will have to leave behind."

Marvelous, thought Marmalade, *no music to listen to. No games to play. This is going to be great fun.* "What about Biscuit? Will I have to leave him there?" she asked. Biscuit looked horrified.

"No dear, Biscuit will be fine," assured Prudence.

"Pity," said Marmalade, smiling down at her ferret.

"Very funny," replied Biscuit.

Marmalade opened up her rucksack, took out her school books, and set them on the kitchen table. She then opened the fridge (which had unplugged itself and was in the process of walking out the kitchen into the hall) and took out two bottles of water, some apples, cheese, and some slices of cold ham and chicken. From a cupboard under the sink she took some potato chips and two chocolate cereal bars. "This should be enough for both of us," she said to herself. Then she went up to her room and brought down her spell book, which she also put into her rucksack.

When she had finished packing, her aunts sat her down to explain what to do.

"Remember, the sooner you find Beatticus Twigg the better," said Winifred.

"What does he look like?" asked Marmalade, starting to feel very, very nervous.

"We don't really know, dear. We have never seen him," answered Prudence, "but there will be someone on The Other Side who will be able to guide you."

"Remember, Morlockins is a very serious thing, Marmalade," said Winifred. "It has only happened a few times in thousands of years, so speed is of the essence. But I wouldn't be surprised if Beatticus and those who live on The Other Side already know about it. News like this travels very fast throughout the witch community, and I dare say that Beatticus is probably expecting a visit from someone."

Marmalade was starting to wish that this was a dream and that very soon she would wake up and it would be Saturday morning.

"Why can't Beatticus just come through the Portal to our house if he already knows what has happened?" asked Biscuit.

"Good point," said Marmalade, looking at her aunts.

"Simply because Beatticus will not interfere unless he is asked to," replied Prudence.

"And it has to be done in person," added Winifred. "Now, are you ready?"

"As ready as I will ever be to go through a Portal to some strange place I have never been before," answered Marmalade.

Her aunts then shooed the cooker out of the way and began chanting a strange incantation that Marmalade had never heard before. Almost at once an inky black door appeared in the wall, which seemed to shimmer like an oil stain on water.

"Time to go," said her aunts.

"Don't worry, I will look after her," replied Biscuit, trying to reassure Winifred and Prudence.

"That is the one thing that DOES worry me," answered Prudence wearily.

Marmalade lifted Biscuit in her arms and turned to face her aunts. "I will be back as soon as I can. Just look after Mum," she said.

"We will, dear, we will," replied Winifred.

She then gave both her aunts a kiss and a hug. "Ready, Biscuit?"

"If I say no, can I stay here?"

"Mmm, let me think," answered Marmalade. "No."

"Thought not," said Biscuit. "Okay, as they say in the Nike ad, let's do it."

Biscuit put his paws tightly over his face as Marmalade took a deep breath, closed her eyes, and stepped into the Portal.

Chapter Five

Immediately Marmalade could feel the warmth of the sun on her face and hear the sound of birds singing. She opened one eye and looked around, and what she saw took her breath away. This was the most beautiful place she had ever been. She was surrounded on all sides by lush green meadows covered in flowers that were every color you could imagine, and some that you couldn't. In the distance there was a forest that seemed to go on for miles and miles, and beyond that there were great snowcapped mountains. The sky was a deep blue, and not a cloud was to be seen. Dotted here and there amongst the meadows were small whitewashed cottages with thatched roofs, and what looked like woolly cows, munching on the grass.

Marmalade could also hear running water as if they were close to a river or stream, but couldn't quite make out where it was.

"Are we there yet?" asked Biscuit.

"Well, let me put it like this," answered Marmalade. "We are definitely not in the kitchen."

Biscuit lowered his paws. "Wow, this is nice," he said, looking around as Marmalade set him on the grass. "There is just one thing, though. How do we get back?"

"Through the same Portal, I suppose," replied Marmalade.

"You mean the one that is disappearing," said Biscuit, pointing over his shoulder.

Marmalade looked, and saw that the Portal they had just come through was now the size of a melon, and as they watched, it got smaller and smaller until it disappeared altogether.

"Now what?" asked Biscuit.

"I have absolutely no idea," replied Marmalade, "but I'm sure someone will be able to get us home. Anyway, we will worry about that later. In the meantime, we better try to find somebody who can tell us how to find Beatticus Twigg, so we will head for the nearest cottage."

As they walked, Marmalade felt very peaceful strolling through the meadow, and not in the slightest bit nervous. All around her she could see butterflies dancing on the breeze. The air was full of the scent of flowers and the sound of bees buzzing and crickets chirping as they called to one another. It was as if the place itself took all your worries away and replaced them with a sense of excitement and wonder.

As they approached the nearest cottage, she could just make out the small figure of someone tending a garden, and as they got closer she could see that it was a very small, very old-looking man with a white shirt, a black waistcoat, and a pure white beard, which appeared to be tucked into the waistband of his red three-quarter-length trousers. The front of the cottage itself was covered in ivy, with roses of every color climbing up the gable ends. All along the front were flower beds, with a vegetable patch on the left-hand side. At the rear Marmalade could just make out paddocks and what looked like henhouses and beehives.

"Hello!" she called when she was sure that she was close enough for the little man to hear her.

The little man turned to face them and put his hand up to his face to shield his eyes from the sun. "Well, bless my soul," he said in surprise, "if it isn't Marmalade Tuttle." Marmalade was taken aback, as she didn't think that anyone would know her on The Other Side. "Come in, child, and let me have a look at you," chuckled the little man, opening the gate.

Marmalade and Biscuit both stared at each other. "How does he know your name?" whispered Biscuit.

"Beats me," answered Marmalade, shrugging her shoulders.

"Well, this is a pleasant surprise," said the little man as Marmalade and Biscuit stood in front of him. "We weren't expecting you to come. My, oh my, how you have grown, and Biscuit here as well. You know, we all thought that it would be Winifred or Prudence who would pass through, but I must say it makes a lovely change to see one of our younger witches. Let me introduce myself," the little man continued. "My name is Algenon Thaddeus Snowbeard, at your service, but folks around here just call me Snowy."

"Sorry, have we met before?" asked Marmalade.

Snowy laughed. "Some time ago," he said, "when you were only a few days old. I attended your naming ceremony, but never mind that now. Let's go inside and you can tell me all about what has happened to poor Imelda. The Morlockins, I hear, but don't worry. If anyone can help, it is Beatticus. You as well, Biscuit, in you go, in you go, just mind your head, and we will talk about what we can do to help your poor mother."

Chapter Six

Marmalade had to duck down as she and Biscuit made their way through the tiny door into the cottage. From the outside, it seemed quite small, but inside it seemed to be twice the size. Marmalade followed as Snowy led them through the living room, down the hall, and into the kitchen.

The kitchen was like an old country kitchen that you would see in a magazine. There was a big stove, a large fire, and a table and chairs, albeit very small. There was a Welsh dresser that was stacked full of plates, bowls, and cups, and a large sink and draining board. The rear window looked over the paddocks, henhouses and beehives, and everywhere there were vases full of the most beautifully scented flowers.

"Sit, sit," said Snowy, "and tell me all that has happened."

Marmalade sat down on a very small chair, with Biscuit lying at her feet, but as she sat, the strangest thing happened; the chair started to grow until it fitted her perfectly. "Cool," she said.

Snowy could see the look on Marmalade's face and grinned at her. "Like it, do you? One of my little inventions. Now, tell me what has happened to Imelda."

Marmalade cleared her throat and told Snowy everything that she knew. About coming home from school and finding her two aunts in a terrible state, screeching and wailing and running around the house, and about her mother lying in bed with obvious signs of Morlockins, and every now and again, Biscuit would interrupt to add some detail of his own. As he listened,

Snowy would "Tut, tut" and shake his head occasionally, followed by a "Dear me, dear me."

"And then I was sent here to find this Beatticus Twigg bloke for a cure, and that's about it, really," Marmalade stated.

"Sounds like the Morlockins alright," said Snowy, "but if there is anyone who can sort it out, it's Beatticus."

"So where do we go to find him?" asked Marmalade.

"That's the thing," answered Snowy, scratching his beard, "Beatticus is not that easy to find. Mostly he lives up in the mountains so that he can keep an eye, so to speak, but there is no guarantee that he is there all the time. A bit of a wanderer is Beatticus. He could pop up any place whenever you least expect him."

"Well, that's just great," said Marmalade sarcastically. "So where do we start?"

"Well, in my experience, the best place to start is at the very beginning. So it would be my reckoning that the first thing to do is to go to his cabin in the mountains and see if he is there. If he's not, then all we can do is look for him."

"But that will take ages," protested Marmalade. "Can't you just, I don't know, summon him or something?"

"Summon Beatticus!" Snowy said in astonishment. "You just can't summon Beatticus, Marmalade. He's not a servant to be called upon. Bless me, child, he is the greatest wizard that has ever lived, not some sort of dog."

"Sorry," said Marmalade, looking very sheepish.

"Anyway, the darkings will be here soon, so there is nothing that we can do until morntime."

Marmalade sighed and looked down at Biscuit. "I have a feeling that we could be here awhile."

"Doesn't matter," replied Biscuit. "I had nothing planned anyway."

Marmalade smiled.

Chapter Seven

Snowy rose from his seat and moved towards a large black pot that was hanging on a chain above the fire. "Ready yet, are we?" he asked, and for a moment Marmalade thought that he was talking to her.

Not quite," replied the pot. "Another five minutes."

"Good, good," Snowy said.

"Well, if we can have a talking gate and post-box, I shouldn't be surprised that you have talking pots," Marmalade said to Snowy.

"Handy, it is." Snowy smiled. "Lets you know when things are done," he continued, reaching for plates and bowls from a shelf on the dresser.

"It smells delicious," said Marmalade. "What is it?"

"A specialty of mine. The recipe was given to me a long, long time ago by a leprechaun from the Emerald Isle, and I added one or two ingredients of my own. But it's the rumble berries that make all the difference."

"What are rumble berries?" asked Biscuit.

"Just whatever you want them to be," replied Snowy. "Tonight we are having Irish stew along with honey and clover bread, so the rumble berries will taste like lamb."

"Bread's done," said the stove as it opened its door, and a loaf of bread flew through the air, landing perfectly on the bread board on the table. Marmalade ducked just in time.

"Stew, too," said the pot.

Snowy ladled the stew into the bowls and cut some slices of

bread. "Well, tuck in, both of you, and there is plenty left if you want seconds."

Marmalade and Biscuit ate as much as they could until they both felt completely full.

"That was lovely, and not too hot," said Marmalade.

"The bread was delicious," said Biscuit. "I might take some back with me."

"Can't do that," replied Snowy. "Remember, nothing from this world can pass over into yours, not even a loaf of honey and clover bread."

As he finished speaking, it suddenly became very dark, and all the candles in the little cottage lit themselves, spreading a warm yellow glow throughout the kitchen. "Well, if we are all finished, it is time to wash up," said Snowy.

"Yes, finished, thank you," replied Marmalade. "I will wash the dishes." She was just about to start clearing the dishes away when they leapt off the table into the sink, closely followed by the pot that was hanging over the fire. In no time at all, they had all washed themselves and jumped back onto the shelf that they came from. "That is so cool," said Marmalade in amazement. "I definitely want some of those to take home." Snowy looked at her, grinned, and shook his head. "I can't take anything home, can I? Damn and bother," she continued.

Chapter Eight

Snowy moved from the kitchen into the sitting room at the front of the house, closely followed by Marmalade and Biscuit. A large fire was roaring in the grate. Snowy sat down in his favourite armchair, kicked off his shoes, and lit his clay pipe, which he carried in the pocket of his waistcoat. Marmalade and Biscuit sat down on a very large, very comfortable settee in front of the window overlooking the meadow where they had arrived through the Portal.

All around the walls were old brown photos of people that Marmalade took to be Snowy's relatives or friends. Above the fireplace was a cuckoo clock and a painting of a beautiful young woman who looked very like Aunt Prudence, only a lot younger. Marmalade looked for a TV or music centre of some sort, but evidently there was none. Sitting along the back wall, however, opposite the fireplace, was a large cabinet with glass doors, which appeared to contain Snowy's best china and a collection of different shaped pipes.

"How long have you known my mum and my aunts?" asked Marmalade.

"Bless me, child, all of their lives," replied Snowy, blowing a cloud of bluish green smoke into the air. "I was at their naming ceremonies as well, and your father's. That was a very long time ago, but I still like to keep in touch whenever I can. I had quite a soft spot for your Aunt Prudence. She was a real beauty back then. That's her on the wall. Your mum painted that and gave it to me to remind me of her, and I wasn't the only one, believe me. Quite a lot of wizards and warlocks tried to woo Prudence, but she would have none of it. She was just happy to stay on her side of the Portal with her sisters, whereas I didn't want to leave here, so it all fizzled out in the end. Pity, though, as I think she would have made a wonderful wife." Marmalade could see the twinkle in Snowy's eyes as he spoke about Prudence and stared at her portrait.

"Is it true that my dad is descended from Merlin?"

"There are those that say so, and I have no reason to doubt them. But I dare say Beatticus could tell you when we find him."

"It would be really great if it was true," Marmalade said, "because that would mean that I would be as well."

"I suppose it would," replied Snowy. "Merlin was one of the greats, nearly as great as Beatticus, which is as it should be, seeing as how it was Beatticus who taught him."

"Do you ever see my dad?" asked Marmalade, "'Cause Mum doesn't really talk about him, what he was like or where he is or anything like that, and whenever I ask, all she ever says is she will tell me when I am older, and she has made my aunts promise not to mention him, either."

Snowy blew a cloud of white smoke from his pipe that raced up the chimney in the shape of a galloping horse, and he looked at Marmalade. "Your dad is a great wizard and a great friend to Beatticus, one of the few that he would ask for advice or trust. He left your side as he was disillusioned with what was happening to the planet and how man folk were treating it. A follower of the Old Ways, your dad is. He believes in treating all living things with respect, no matter what they are, trees or birds or insects, fish or beasts, it doesn't matter to him. So when he saw what was happening and how men and their machines were ruining the very things he loved, he decided to leave and come here. He tried to persuade your mum to come, of course, but she wouldn't, as she wanted you to grow up in a modern world with normal friends and normal schooling. Your dad is still here and travels all over our side as a sort of ambassador for Beatticus, settling disputes and administering healing to those that need it. Take it from me, Marmalade, your father is a great man, and you should be very proud of him."

Marmalade could feel the tears welling up in her eyes. "I am proud of him," she whispered, "and who knows, maybe I will get to see him while I am here."

"Maybe, maybe," said Snowy kindly.

"How old are you, Snowy? If you don't mind me asking," said Biscuit.

"Biscuit!" scolded Marmalade. "It's very rude to ask something like that."

"Sorry, but I was only wondering."

Snowy laughed. "No harm done. I don't mind telling you both that I am now in my eight hundredth year."

"Wow! That is old," said Biscuit, and then said, "Sorry" again as he saw Marmalade giving him one of her stern looks.

Snowy roared with laughter and blew his nose on his handkerchief. "Yes, you are quite right, Biscuit, I am very old indeed," he said, "but quite young compared to some, and a mere child compared to many, including Beatticus."

"Where exactly did Beatticus come from?" asked Marmalade.

Snowy smoked on his pipe and this time blew a cloud of reddish orange smoke into the air, which went into a circle, then a square, then a triangle, and then disappeared in a shower of tiny sparkles.

"Only Beatticus knows that, and he's not for telling folk," answered Snowy. "All I do know is that he is the oldest of all the witches, wizards, and warlocks, but as to what age he is or where he came from, who can say? But whatever is wrong with Imelda, he will cure it."

As Marmalade looked out the window, she saw that the woolly cows were coming in from the fields and settling down in one of the paddocks at the rear of Snowy's house. The sky was turning a pitch black, but was illuminated by millions of the brightest stars that she had ever seen, and much to her surprise, there was an actual blue moon in the sky.

"Bedtime, bedtime," said the cuckoo clock, and Snowy got up after emptying his pipe into the fire.

"Let me show you where you will sleep," he said as he led Marmalade and Biscuit to a room at the rear of the house. "I hope you will find this to your liking, and try to get a good night's sleep, as we could have a long couple of days in front of us."

"Are you coming with us?" asked Biscuit.

"Of course I am," replied Snowy. "You didn't think I would let a niece of Prudence's go wandering around here all on her own, did you?"

"I'm glad," said Marmalade, sleepily.

"Me too," added Biscuit.

Snowy said his goodnights, and Marmalade and Biscuit lay down on top of the bed. It was the softest, most comfortable bed that Marmalade had ever slept in, and it wasn't long before she was sound asleep, dreaming of talking pots, leprechauns, flying loaves of bread, her mum, and her dad.

Chapter Nine

The next morning, after a very good night's sleep, Marmalade was awakened by a hen tapping at her window.

"Good morning," said the hen. "It is time to get up."

"Er, thank you very much," replied Marmalade, stretching and yawning.

"You're welcome," answered the hen, and off it went.

Things certainly are a lot different around here, Marmalade thought as she looked around the room. The room itself wasn't that big. Around the walls were holders with candles in them. A window overlooked the henhouses, and in the far corner were a wicker chair and a wooden table. Next to the table was a stand with a large jug and bowl, which were full of hot water. Marmalade got up, washed her hands and face, and made her way down to the kitchen, where Snowy and Biscuit were already making breakfast.

"Morning, Marmalade. Scrambled eggs, mushrooms, and oat bread toast alright with you?" asked Snowy.

"Yes, sounds lovely," she replied.

Biscuit pushed a glass towards her with pink-looking milky stuff in it. "You have got to try this," he said. "It is delicious and ice cold, just what you need on a warm morning like this."

Marmalade took a sip. "Very refreshing. What is it?"

"Milk from the Lambrils," replied Biscuit, "those woolly-looking cow things."

"Oh, is that what they are?"

"Great things, Lambrils," replied Snowy. "Give us milk and wool they do, and meat as well, if you have a mind to eat it. Me, though, I don't eat the meat, mostly 'cause I haven't the heart to kill any of the Lambrils."

Marmalade sat down at the table, and Snowy served the breakfast.

"So what is our plan of action for today?" she asked in between mouthfuls of food.

"Well, I think that we should head for Beatticus' cabin. It's a long way, mind you, so we will have to take some food with us, and we may even have to sleep out a couple of nights, depending on how fast we can travel," answered Snowy.

"That's great!" said Biscuit. "Camping out under the stars. I love doing that."

"When have you ever camped out under the stars?" asked Marmalade.

"Well, I haven't actually, but I'm sure it's great fun," answered Biscuit.

"Oh, by the way," Marmalade said to Snowy, "that reminds me, I brought some food with me from home," and she started to empty her rucksack and set the food on the kitchen table.

"Doesn't look very appetizing," said Snowy, poking at it with his finger. "We can take the fruit and the water, but the rest of it, whatever it is, we will leave here. I have prepared enough for the journey, for all of us."

After breakfast was over and the dishes had again washed

themselves, it was time to get started. Marmalade went to the loo and then put on her rucksack. Snowy had an old green canvas rucksack and a pouch hanging from his belt in which he carried tobacco and a spare pipe. Biscuit had nothing. Then they all went out of the house by the front door, and Marmalade and Biscuit waited while Snowy gathered the Lambrils around the house and told them where he was going.

"Right, let's go find Beatticus then," said Snowy, closing the gate behind him.

Chapter Ten

It was another beautiful morning as the three travelers set off. The sun was shining, and again there was not a cloud in the sky.

"Do you always tell the house and the Lambrils where you are going?" asked Marmalade, walking beside Snowy.

"Aye, always," answered Snowy, "just to stop them fretting, so to speak. They say that folk get very attached to their homes and animals, but what they forget is that it works the other way round, too, and homes and animals get very attached to the folk that look after them. I always let them know when I am going away for a spell, just to reassure them that I am coming back."

"I never thought of it like that," answered Marmalade. "I must try and remember that when I get home."

They had walked for quite some distance when they came to a small track that ran through the meadows.

"If we turn left here, it will take us to the main path that leads to the river," said Snowy. As they walked along the path, Snowy told Marmalade that this side of the Portal was called Caldor, and he explained why Beatticus Twigg had created it, while Biscuit ran on ahead exploring. "In the olden days, witches and wizards and the like were not accepted very well on your side of the Portal," he explained. "Folk viewed them with a great deal of fear and suspicion and blamed them for everything bad that happened. If crops failed, it was a witch's fault, or if cattle died, or if a village were hit by a plague or disease, then it was a curse brought about by a witch, and so folk would start having witch hunts, and a lot of witches were persecuted and burned. Some that were burned weren't even witches at all, but had maybe fallen out with their neighbor, and so the neighbor branded them as such, just to get revenge. Dark days those were, Marmalade, believe me, so Beatticus decided to create this place as a sort of sanctuary that the likes of us could come to in order to escape persecution."

Marmalade listened intently to what Snowy was telling her as they walked along. "Did it take long to build Caldor?" she asked, chewing on a stalk of grass.

"A fair while, and all the witching folk helped as best as they could, but even so it took several centuries of your time, and to be honest, if it hadn't been for the great skill and powers of Beatticus, it probably wouldn't be finished yet."

"None of my friends even knows I'm a witch," said Marmalade, "or my mum, or my aunts."

"Sometimes it's best to keep it like that," Snowy said, "but I dare say that things are a lot better on your side of the Portal now. I mean, I can't see any of your friends tying you to a stake and setting fire to you, can you?"

"No, definitely not, although having said that, there are some girls in my school who I wouldn't mind seeing it happen to," she replied.

"Marmalade Tuttle!" Snowy laughed.

They hadn't walked very far when Biscuit came running back to them. "There is a river up ahead, but I don't know how we are going to get across it. I couldn't find a bridge or a boat or anything."

"Don't you go worrying yourself about that," replied Snowy. "We will wait for the Narkles to appear, and they will take us."

"I take it you are going to tell us what a Narkle is," Marmalade said, looking puzzled.

Snowy chuckled. "Nope, that would spoil the surprise, so you are just going to have to be patient and see for yourself."

When they got to the river, they clambered down a gently sloping bank and sat down on the gravel, and while Snowy filled and lit his pipe, Marmalade and Biscuit went for a look around. "Don't stray far, you two," said Snowy, lying back on the grass.

"We won't," replied Marmalade, following Biscuit a short distance along the river's edge. The river itself was quite large, and it did appear to be a long way to the other bank, but it flowed very slowly. Marmalade could see insects and flies buzzing close to the surface of the water, which was broken once in a while by a hungry fish leaping up to grab a meal, and further upstream she could just make out some ducks, with their tails pointed to the sky as they searched for plants along the river bed.

Biscuit decided to have a paddle, while Marmalade began playing "Ducks and Drakes" by skimming flat stones across the surface of the water. She was about to skim her third stone when suddenly a huge catfish reared its head up out of the water no more than three feet from where she was standing. Biscuit let out a yell and in one bound was back on the riverbank at Marmalade's feet.

"Oy you!" shouted the catfish crossly. "Yes, you! Stop chucking stones into the water. The young fish are all terrified."

Marmalade stood with her mouth gaping wide open in surprise, and Biscuit hid behind her legs. "I'm, eh, very sorry," she stammered. "I didn't think I was doing any harm, and I certainly didn't mean to frighten anyone."

"Well, maybe you should think about us fish before you start throwing stones into a river. After all, how would you like it if we all came round to where you live and threw stones at you, eh?" With that, he disappeared back under the water.

Marmalade stood for a while, totally amazed. *That is the first time ever I have been told off by a fish*, she thought, and then she went back and sat down beside Snowy with Biscuit following her.

"This is a very strange place," said Biscuit.

"It's very peaceful here," Marmalade said to Snowy, trying to appear composed.

"Aye, my favourite place this is, except for cantankerous catfish," he answered, smiling. Marmalade felt herself blushing with embarrassment. "Many an hour I have spent here just whiling away the time, or trying to catch some of those catfish," he continued.

"After we cross the river, where do we go?" Marmalade changed the subject.

"Well, we are not crossing the river yet. We have to go quite some distance upstream to nearer the source first before we can cross, but that won't take too long with the Narkles helping us."

"I wish you would tell me what a Narkle is," said Marmalade.

"All in good time, Marmalade, all in good time," answered Snowy, blowing different-colored smoke rings into the air.

Marmalade lay down on the shingle, as Biscuit had summoned up the courage to wander off again, and began to wonder about her mum back home. "I hope my mum is okay."

"She will be fine, Marmalade," Snowy said reassuringly, "you'll see."

Marmalade smiled and lay on her back staring up at the clear blue sky, still not believing where she was and what was happening. "Snowy? Have you ever seen anyone with Morlockins before?"

"Not I, but I have heard stories from the past of others, not very many, mind, who have crossed over and sought the help of Beatticus."

"And was he able to cure them okay?"

"Aye, they all passed back completely cured, so stop worrying your young head about it. Winifred and Prudence will take good care of Imelda until you get back with the cure, or who knows, maybe Beatticus will cross over to give the cure himself, but whatever happens, she will be fine."

Marmalade felt reassured by what Snowy had said, and as she lay on the riverbank listening to the sound of the water lapping on the bank and feeling the warmth of the sun on her face, she began to doze off.

Chapter Eleven

Marmalade wasn't sure how long she had been dozing before she was suddenly awakened by a tremendous gushing, thundering sound, and larger and larger waves appeared on the surface of the river. Marmalade began to get very concerned. "What's happening?" she shouted to make herself heard above the roar.

"Nothing to get frightened about," answered Snowy, detecting the fear in Marmalade's voice. "Narkles are coming, is all."

Biscuit raced along the shingle and bounced into Marmalade's arms, visibly shaking. Marmalade put him into her rucksack and followed Snowy back up the bank away from the water's edge. "Safer we are up here," he said. "Narkles tend to throw up quite a bit of water when they appear."

Marmalade stood beside Snowy and gazed upstream. The river was getting choppier and choppier, and all along the surface, birds took to the skies, squawking in alarm to escape whatever was approaching. As Marmalade stood watching, a huge wave began to make its way towards them from upstream, and behind it, she could make out what appeared to be a number of very large dragons, swimming in its wake.

"Watch out for the wave," yelled Snowy, "or you might get more than just your feet wet!" He laughed.

Marmalade was rooted to the spot, spellbound, as the Narkles came closer and closer. The wave had made its way over the bank and soaked her up to her knees, but Marmalade didn't seem to notice.

As the wave passed, five Narkles appeared. They were huge. Each one was around fifty feet long and looked exactly like dragons that Marmalade had seen so many times in storybooks. Their heads were enormous, with disc-like eyes and long protruding mouths that were filled with rows of razor-sharp teeth. On top of their heads they each had two horns, and their skin was covered in thick green scales. Instead of feet, they all had huge flippers, two on each side of their bodies. Smoke billowed from their nostrils, and Marmalade thought they were the most magnificent creatures she had ever seen.

Biscuit had burrowed down into Marmalade's rucksack, not daring to look and wishing that he was back home in the garden.

"Wow!" said Marmalade. "They look just like dragons. Are they dangerous?"

"No," answered Snowy, "they're water dragons and mostly eat plants or fish, but they can get a bit jittery around strangers, so you stay here while I go and talk with them."

Marmalade did as she was told, while Snowy made his way down the bank to talk to the Narkles.

Biscuit popped his head out of the rucksack. "Are they gone yet?"

"No, they're still here," answered Marmalade, "but Snowy says they are mostly vegetarians and not dangerous, so you can come out."

Biscuit climbed out of the rucksack and sat on Marmalade's lap. "Big, aren't they," he said, hardly daring to look at the creatures.

"Very big. They should get us to the source of the river in no time."

Just then, one of the Narkles saw Biscuit sitting on Marmalade's knee and let out an almighty roar that was so loud, Marmalade and Biscuit had to cover their ears from the noise.

"What's wrong, Snowy?" shouted Marmalade.

"Seems that one of the Narkles is scared of young Biscuit there," replied Snowy, shouting as loud as he could, "and thinks that he is some sort of mythical creature that has come to destroy them."

Biscuit couldn't believe what he was hearing. "That huge dragon is afraid of me?"

"Bring Biscuit down here to let the Narkles see him better," shouted Snowy. Marmalade carried Biscuit down the bank and stood beside Snowy. It was only when she was this close to the Narkles did she really begin to appreciate how big they were. Snowy took Biscuit from her and lifted him up for the Narkles to smell. "Hopefully this will calm them down," he said.

All the Narkles bent their long necks down to sniff Biscuit, who, it must be said, was enjoying the thought of these mighty beasts being afraid of him. "Seems they're fine now," said Snowy, setting Biscuit back down on the shingle.

"Will they take us?" asked Marmalade.

"Oh, they will take us alright," replied Snowy, "but they say that the river is in flood further upstream, with melt water coming from the mountains, so it might take a lot longer than we thought." Marmalade reached out to stroke the neck of the Narkle that was closest to her, but it shied away and engulfed her in a cloud of smoke. "Careful, Marmalade," said Snowy, "remember what I said. They can be very nervous of strangers."

Marmalade reached out again, and this time the Narkle reached down to let her stroke it. "Good boy," she said. "I'm not going to hurt you."

"Actually, that one is a girl." Snowy laughed. "Let's get our stuff together and climb up."

Marmalade grabbed her rucksack, fixed it on her back, and lifted Biscuit in her arms. The Narkle that she had stroked lowered its neck, and she clambered onto it, followed by Snowy.

"Best hold on tight," said Snowy. "Narkles can travel very fast when they have a mind to."

Marmalade held on for all she was worth, and with a great roar and a swish of their mighty tails, which sent a cloud of spray into the air, the Narkles set off.

Chapter Twelve

Sitting on top of the Narkle as it sped through the water was without doubt the most exhilarating thing that Marmalade had ever experienced, and it took all of her strength to keep from falling off.

Biscuit, on the other hand, was not enjoying himself one little bit, and after a short while felt his tummy starting to heave, so he crawled back into the rucksack. "Let me know when we get to where we are going. I think I will sleep this one out," he said, looking decidedly unwell. Snowy and Marmalade both laughed as Biscuit's head disappeared from view.

"How many Narkles are there?" asked Marmalade.

"Just these ones," answered Snowy. "They swim all along the rivers before heading out into the great ocean, and then they can be gone for months, so we were lucky to catch them."

"I hope we're not keeping them back," said Marmalade.

"No, no," answered Snowy, "Narkles come and go as they please and have plenty of days yet before they must reach the ocean."

"Are they the only dragons?" asked Marmalade.

"Down here they are," answered Snowy, "but up in the mountains there are others. Ones that fly, like the ones in your book, I expect, but even they are fairly tame now and don't cause too much of a problem. Sometimes they will fly down and take the odd Lambril, but not that often. Beatticus doesn't like it, and it doesn't pay to get on his bad side, as they found out a long time ago when he took away their fire.

Now they mostly behave themselves, so they got it back in the end."

Riding on the Narkle was like being on the fastest roller-coaster that had ever been built. The riverbank was just a blur as they sped past, heading farther and farther upstream, but even so the mountains that were the source of the great river didn't seem to be getting any closer, and Marmalade mentioned this to Snowy.

"Aye, it's a long way to the mountains," replied Snowy. "We will be lucky if we make it before the darkings, so I suppose we had better stop soon for something to eat."

"Good," replied Marmalade, "'cause I'm starving."

Snowy shouted something to the Narkles that Marmalade didn't understand, and they nodded their great heads. Soon they were landing on a stretch of sand by the river. Marmalade and Snowy jumped off the great beast, and Snowy took off his rucksack and laid it on the ground beside him.

Biscuit appeared out of Marmalade's rucksack and looked around. "Are we there yet?" he inquired, preening his whiskers and belching loudly.

"Not yet," replied Snowy. "We have just stopped for lunch is all, if you want some."

"Er, no, thank you," replied Biscuit. "Maybe later when my stomach isn't doing cartwheels I will be able to manage something. In the meantime I think I will just lie down for a while."

Snowy smiled and winked at Marmalade. "First time I ever saw a green-looking ferret." He laughed.

Snowy took two tiny baskets out of his rucksack and set them on the ground. He then clapped his hands together and touched each basket with the forefinger of his right hand. Immediately, each one grew in size until Marmalade could open her basket up and peer inside. There was fruit, sandwiches, what appeared to be chicken legs, containers of rumble berries, home-cooked biscuits, different slices of cake, and a large jug of Lambrils' milk.

"Now that is what I call a picnic," said Marmalade, taking out some chicken and fruit and pouring out a glass of milk.

As Marmalade and Snowy ate their lunch and Biscuit dozed, the Narkles would occasionally dive to the bottom of the river and reappear with great mouthfuls of weeds and the odd fish. Then they would throw back their long necks, raise their heads, and blow great columns of white smoke into the air, as if they were letting the rest of the animals along the riverbank know they were there.

Marmalade ate as much as she could, but the food in her basket didn't seem to be getting any less. When she was full, she closed the lid and lay back on the sand.

Snowy lit his pipe. "I hope when this is over and Imelda is cured that you will come and visit," he said.

"I would love to, if that's okay with you," replied Marmalade.

"Course it is, as long as your mother and aunts don't object."

"They won't mind, but I would have to wait until school holidays so that I could stay for a few days. I was supposed to be going into town today to the movies with my friends, but little did I know that I would be here instead, riding along a river on the back of a dragon." She laughed.

"Ah, but you can still go with your friends," said Snowy, tapping his nose.

"I don't see how," Marmalade said.

"Very simple," said Snowy, tapping the tobacco out of his pipe against the heel of his boot. "When we send you back through the Portal, we will just send you back to the same time that you left, which means that you could spend as long as you liked here and go back five minutes after you left."

"That means I can visit whenever I like."

"Exactly, and stay as long as you want, too."

"Then I definitely will come and visit," said Marmalade.

"Good, I would like that," replied Snowy. He walked over and started to tickle Biscuit's nose with a blade of grass until the ferret sneezed and opened his eyes. "Time to get going again, if you think you can manage it," he said.

"Do we have to? Couldn't we just walk or get a bus or something?" asked Biscuit.

"'Fraid not," answered Snowy, shrinking the baskets and putting them back into his rucksack. "There are no buses, and walking would take too long, and we have to find Beatticus as soon as we can for Imelda's sake, don't you think?"

"I suppose so," agreed Biscuit, sighing and climbing into Marmalade's rucksack.

Snowy and Marmalade climbed aboard the Narkle, and when they were settled, Snowy gave a shout like an Eskimo leading a team of huskies. The Narkles gave a great roar in response, and once again they were speeding towards the mountains.

Chapter Thirteen

As they sped along, Marmalade could see that they were fast approaching the forest. "When we get to the forest, we will have to start walking," said Snowy. "The river there gets too narrow and shallow for the Narkles."

"Looks as if it's starting to get dark," replied Marmalade.

"Aye that it is, so we best make camp when we reach the forest, if we can find a good spot."

They continued to travel upstream until it was obvious that the Narkles couldn't go any farther. They were at the outer edge of the forest, which Marmalade thought looked very dark and very foreboding. The Narkles slowed to a crawl and made their way over to the bank. Marmalade and Snowy jumped down.

"Thank you very much for the ride," said Marmalade to her beast.

The great Narkle lowered its head so that Marmalade was able to scratch it behind the ears, and for the briefest of seconds it looked as if it actually smiled at her. Snowy was talking with the biggest of the Narkles, obviously the head of the group, and then with another great roar they left, leaving the three travelers on the riverbank, watching as they disappeared downstream into the inky blackness of the night.

"We best make camp," said Snowy as he started to clear the ground of broken twigs and leaves.

Marmalade set down her rucksack to help. She felt sad that the Narkles had gone, and promised herself that she would make a point of seeing them again some day. She also suddenly felt a bit vulnerable, standing in a strange forest, in a strange land, with nothing that was the slightest bit familiar to her.

Biscuit appeared beside her. "Are you okay?" he said. "You look a bit down in the dumps."

"No, I'm fine," she answered, smiling at her friend. "What about you? Are you going to try and eat some supper?"

"Yes, I feel a lot better now that we are back on dry land. In fact, I could eat a whole Lambril between two slices of bread." Biscuit laughed.

Marmalade picked him up and hugged him. "I'm glad you are here with me."

"Me too," replied Biscuit. "Me too."

Chapter Fourteen

Snowy and Marmalade cleared an area around some trees. Snowy was taking two sleeping bags out of his rucksack when Marmalade heard what sounded like a hissing noise. She looked around, trying to see through the trees, but it was so dark she could see nothing. The hissing continued, and then suddenly she felt something hit her on the back of the head. She looked down and saw a pine cone lying at her feet.

"Someone just hit me on the head with a pine cone," she said to Snowy, "and I can hear hissing."

"So can I," added Biscuit nervously.

"It's the Hoppalongers," replied Snowy. "Best just to ignore them, and they will go away."

"Are they dangerous?" asked Marmalade. "'Cause they sound very angry."

"No, they're not dangerous. They're elfin creatures that live in the forest, and they can be very malicious when they put a mind to it."

"Why are they called Hoppalongers?" asked Biscuit.

"Probably on account of their only having one leg," replied Snowy, "and having to hop along to get around."

"Makes sense, I suppose," said Marmalade.

Snowy placed the sleeping bags on the ground and started to make a fire to cook a meal. As soon as the fire was lit, a chorus of whispered voices resounded all around the campsite.

"Leave this place, leave this place," the voices cackled.

"Seems the Hoppalongers don't want us here," said Marmalade, hugging her knees up to her chest.

"They don't like anyone coming into the forest. They think they own it and no one else should be here, but they'll soon learn that I AM NOT LEAVING." Snowy shouted this last part, looking around the forest, so that the Hoppalongers would hear, and for a moment it appeared that it did the trick, for there was an eerie silence. Then the voices returned, only louder.

"Leave this forest. Now!"

Marmalade looked nervously at Snowy, who got to his feet.

"We are only travelers and mean no harm. This forest belongs to everyone, and all are entitled to pass through!" he shouted. Again there was a short silence.

"You have been warned!" said one of the voices menacingly. "On your own heads be it."

Marmalade then heard the sound of something moving away through the bushes.

Snowy knelt down, put some water into the pot, and then added some vegetables and rumble berries. Marmalade and Biscuit settled down on the grass, feeling very uneasy. It was dark now, and the campsite was bathed in the light of the moon, and all around the forest there was silence, except for the sounds of the night creatures scavenging for a meal in the undergrowth, and an owl hooting somewhere off in the trees. Snowy had relit his pipe and sat beside the cooking pot, stirring its contents.

"It's gone very quiet," said Marmalade. "The Hoppalongers must have headed off."

"Oh, they're close by," replied Snowy. "You just can't see them is all." He opened his rucksack and took out some bowls and spoons, along with another jug of Lambrils' milk, which he set on the ground.

"Have we much farther to go?" asked Marmalade.

"A fair way yet, so we should get a good night's sleep and make an early start in the morning."

"What about the Hoppalongers?" asked Biscuit.

"Don't worry about them," replied Snowy, still stirring the pot.

Marmalade looked around the forest, but still couldn't see any sign of the Hoppalongers anywhere. "I wish I could see them," she said, "just to see what they look like."

"Believe me, Marmalade, Hoppalongers are best left where they are."

Soon, the stew was ready, and Snowy ladled it out into the bowls and poured the milk. He also took out some honey bread, which he broke into three pieces, handing a piece each to Marmalade and Biscuit.

"How much stuff have you got in that rucksack? It seems like a bottomless pit!" Marmalade laughed.

"Ah, appearances can be deceptive," answered Snowy, smiling. "Just because something looks small on the outside doesn't necessarily mean it's small on the inside."

Marmalade ate her supper, which was delicious. Even Biscuit managed to eat a plateful. After they were finished, the plates and glasses headed off down to the river to wash themselves, and in no time at all they were back in Snowy's rucksack. The three friends then settled down for the night, cozy inside their sleeping bags. Snowy waved his hand over the fire, which died down to a red glow.

"Don't want to set the forest on fire," he said, zipping up his sleeping bag.

"Definitely not," replied Marmalade. "Imagine what the Hoppalongers would say."

"Goodnight, you two," said Snowy. "Try to get a good night's rest."

"We will," replied Marmalade. "Goodnight."

Chapter Fifteen

The next morning, Marmalade woke up and yawned. It was already starting to get warm, and the forest was full of birdsong. She tried to stretch her arms and legs but found that she couldn't. She lifted her head and looked down at her sleeping bag and found to her horror that she was bound in what appeared to be strands of silk akin to what a spider would spin. Then she heard a piercing laugh.

"Snowy!" she screamed. "I can't move."

Snowy woke up and found that he couldn't move, either. "It's the Hoppalongers," he said. "They think that this is some kind of joke, but they will soon find out that I am not laughing." He struggled to free himself, but soon discovered that the more he struggled, the tighter the silk became. "Just lie still, Marmalade, until I figure out what to do."

Marmalade looked around, straining to see Biscuit, then saw him lying about five feet away to her left with his four paws bound together and looking very scared. She then heard a very high-pitched, squeaky voice.

"Not for moving, are you?" said the voice. "Forest belongs to everyone, does it?"

Marmalade lifted her head and saw a small, grotesque, elflike creature standing on one leg, staring at them. The creature was about four feet tall and was completely naked except for a loincloth around its middle. It had bright green skin and long dark green hair, which reached to its waist. Its eyes were blood red, its ears were pointed as were its teeth, and it did not look one bit friendly, as in its right hand it carried a long spear. In the undergrowth, Marmalade could just make out the shapes of dozens and dozens of similar-looking creatures.

The Hoppalonger looked at the three of them lying helpless on the ground. "Let me introduce myself," he said, sneering at them. "I am Jedemal, ruler of the Hoppalongers and therefore ruler of this forest. You are here without my permission and are therefore trespassing." He then hopped over to where Snowy was lying. "You I know. You are Snowbeard of the Meadows, but you," he said, looking at Marmalade, "you are a stranger to me, as is that beast that you have with you." He pointed at Biscuit with a long bony finger.

Marmalade opened her mouth to say who she was, but before she could say anything, she was interrupted by Snowy. "This forest belongs to everyone, Jedemal, as you well know," he shouted, "and I don't think Beatticus will take too kindly to the daughter of his ambassador being trussed up like a Lambril prepared for slaughter, do you?"

Jedemal looked puzzled. "What do you mean, Snowbeard?" he said, screeching even louder and poking Snowy with his spear. "Are you trying to frighten Jedemal? Or maybe trick old Jedemal?"

"Not I," replied Snowy. "Tell him who you are, Marmalade, and why you are here."

Marmalade took a deep breath to calm her already frayed nerves. "My name is Marmalade Tuttle, and I am here because my mother, Imelda, has Morlockins," she stated, starting to get annoyed rather than frightened.

"You are the Shatlock's daughter?" wailed Jedemal, pulling at his hair as he stood over her.

"That she is," replied Snowy calmly, "and she has crossed over to consult with Beatticus, so if I were you I would release us before Beatticus decides to take away your other leg."

Jedemal let out a loud yell, and immediately the rest of the Hoppalongers appeared from the undergrowth, gathering in a circle around Jedemal. By now, Jedemal was visibly shaking. "Don't just stand there, fools," he shouted. "Untie them; untie them, quickly, quickly." The Hoppalongers did as they were ordered, and as Marmalade was being freed, Jedemal appeared at her side, groveling. "It is sorry I am. I had no idea that you are the great Shatlock's daughter. Please accept my deepest and humblest apologies. If only I had known. I hope you can maybe forget this, er, unfortunate incident and perhaps not mention it to Beatticus or your father. Eh."

"I can forget about it on one condition," answered Marmalade, getting to her feet.

"Of course," replied Jedemal, helping Marmalade up. "Anything, anything, you only have to ask."

"That from now on, you promise to treat anyone who visits this forest with a bit of courtesy, instead of trying to scare them away," said Marmalade, stepping out of her sleeping bag.

"I will, I will.. That I promise, and Jedemal always keeps his promises. So have we reached an understanding? Yes?" he said, addressing all three of them.

"Aye, seems like it," answered Snowy, "if Marmalade is sure."

"I'm sure," said Marmalade. "Just gather up the rest of your people, Jedemal, and be on your way."

Jedemal shouted some orders, turned round, and bowing very low to Marmalade, disappeared into the forest with the rest of the Hoppalongers.

"Well, that was an interesting way to start the day," said Biscuit.

Snowy and Marmalade looked at each other and burst into fits of laughter, and it was then that Marmalade suddenly realized that, for the first time, she had heard her father's name.

"So his name is Shatlock, my father, I mean?"

"Aye, that it is," replied Snowy, gathering up the sleeping bags.

"Strange name," said Marmalade thoughtfully.

"Aye."

Chapter Sixteen

After they had eaten breakfast and packed up, Marmalade, Snowy, and Biscuit headed into the forest. Snowy seemed strangely quiet and appeared to be deep in thought. "Are you okay?" asked Marmalade. "You seem to be miles away."

"Just thinking is all," replied Snowy, filling his pipe.

"What about?"

"Jedemal. Something tells me that we haven't seen the last of him."

"What did you mean when you said that Beatticus would take away his other leg if he didn't free us?"

Snowy stopped, sat down on a fallen tree trunk, and started to light his pipe. Marmalade and Biscuit sat down as well. "Many centuries ago," he began, "the Hoppalongers had two legs, the same as you, and they were the swiftest and most agile of all the creatures in the forest, but they were ruled by a chief called Locklar, who wasn't content with his piece of the forest. He waged a war on the other inhabitants in order to gain more land for his people, and spilled a great deal of blood in the process. Beatticus had hoped that the other forest dwellers would ally together to defeat Locklar, but they didn't. They ended up quarrelling among themselves and couldn't agree as to who would lead them, so in turn they were defeated, one by one. It was only then that Beatticus intervened and put an end to the bloodshed.

"The elders of the Hoppalongers were tried before the Great Council, and as a result, Beatticus returned all the land that Locklar had taken, but he also decided that they had to be punished, so he decreed that Locklar and his people would never again be the swiftest in the forest by removing one of their legs, making it safe for the rest of the forest dwellers.

"Since then the Hoppalongers have been peaceful, but I worry about this one that calls himself Jedemal. Seems like he has been listening to the old ways." Snowy looked at Marmalade and Biscuit sitting quietly beside him, listening intently. "Maybe I am just getting paranoid in my old age," he said, smiling.

"I certainly hope so," said Marmalade.

Snowy got to his feet. "Time to move on. We still have a long ways to go."

As they walked along, Marmalade couldn't help thinking about what Snowy had said about the Hoppalongers, and began to feel a bit sorry for them that Beatticus had taken away one of their legs, but she told herself, if that was his way of punishing them, who was she to judge. After all, she was only twelve, and what did she know about wars and the like?

Her thoughts were suddenly broken by a blood-curdling scream, and in front of her, about ten feet away, she saw Jedemal rush from the trees and launch himself at Snowy, with his spear raised above his head. Snowy suddenly had a sword in his hands and swung it in an arc at Jedemal just as the Hoppalonger jumped into the air to attack. As Jedemal landed on the ground, he appeared unhurt, and Marmalade thought that Snowy had missed, but as she watched, Jedemal fell to the leaf litter, neatly cut in two at the waist. Jedemal's blood seeped into the ground, and his body went from being bright green to blue. Marmalade couldn't believe what she had just seen.

Snowy stood, sword in hand, looking for other signs of danger. Hundreds of Hoppalongers then appeared from the undergrowth and surrounded them. Marmalade was petrified, and Biscuit was cowering behind her legs, whimpering, so she gathered him up in her arms.

One of the Hoppalongers then approached Jedemal's body. He appeared to be a lot younger than Jedemal and a lot broader. He stared at the body lying on the ground and then, to Marmalade's surprise, spat on it. He turned to face Snowy, who raised his sword. "Put up your sword, Snowbeard," said the Hoppalonger. "You have nothing to fear. I am Gormaleer, ruler, now that you have disposed of Jedemal. Your reputation with a sword is well justified, I see."

Snowy lowered his sword very slowly. "What did Jedemal want?" he asked.

"The girl. When he discovered that she was the daughter of Shatlock, he planned to hold her for ransom."

"In exchange for what?" Snowy asked, watching intently every move of the rest of the Hoppalongers.

"The return of our leg and the lands that were won by our forefathers," Gormaleer replied. "Jedemal believed in the old ways, and his head was filled with tales of past battles and past glories. He wanted to be remembered in the lore of our people as the leader who got our leg and lands restored to us and as the one who defeated the great Beatticus. We tried to talk him out of it, but his mind was set."

"And you? What about you, Gormaleer? Do you feel the same?"

"Me? I just want to live in peace, Snowbeard, and rule my people, and if you see Beatticus or Shatlock, tell them that. We do not hold the same views as Jedemal. Now go in peace, my friends, and remember that you are always welcome in the forest," he added.

Gormaleer then turned to face his people, and they began to disperse back into the undergrowth. Marmalade ran after him and grabbed him by the arm.

"Wait! What about Jedemal's body?"

Gormaleer glanced over his shoulder at the body of his old chief lying in the dirt. "Leave it for the forest creatures. As an example," he said, and as quickly as they had arrived, the Hoppalongers disappeared. Marmalade threw herself down on her hands and knees, retching violently as her breakfast spilled onto the forest floor.

Chapter Seventeen

Snowy came and knelt beside her, putting his arm around her shoulders. "Sorry I am that you had to see that," he said. "Here, drink some water."

Marmalade drank as much as she could to rid herself of the taste of acid in her throat. "Where did the sword come from?" she asked. "You don't even have a sword with you."

"It knows when to appear," replied Snowy. "First sign of danger, it appears."

Marmalade drank some more. "Gormaleer said that your reputation with a sword was well known. Is that true?" She spit and wiped the vomit from her chin.

"I didn't always live in the meadows raising Lambrils and tending to flower gardens, Marmalade. Our side of the Portal wasn't always as peaceful as it is now. Battles have been fought here and wrongdoings put right, and that's how it had to be at the beginning. That is all in the past now, though. Ancient history."

"I hope so," said Marmalade, getting to her feet. "I really do hope so." She sat beside Biscuit. "Are you alright?"

"A bit shaken, but I'm okay," he replied. "What about you?"

"I will be fine." She then turned to Snowy. "Can we just get out of here?" she asked.

Snowy nodded his head. "Let's move on."

Marmalade put her rucksack on her back, and no matter how much she tried not to, she had to have a last look at Jedemal, whose body was already starting to wither.

"I would feel better if we buried him," she said.

"Best just to leave him where he is, and do as Gormaleer asks."

"I suppose so," Marmalade conceded, and after taking another drink of water, they again started off.

They walked through the forest for quite some distance with nobody saying a word. Marmalade still was in a state of shock at what had happened, and still felt very guilty that they didn't bury Jedemal, but deep down she knew that Snowy was probably right. Biscuit stayed at Snowy's side instead of going off exploring like he usually would.

Marmalade eventually broke the uneasy silence. "How did you learn to use a sword like that?"

"I had a great teacher," replied Snowy.

"I never thanked you for saving me from Jedemal."

"No need to thank me. I just hope that what happened doesn't make you feel any less of me, or our side of the Portal."

Marmalade gave Snowy a reassuring smile. "No, it doesn't," she replied.

"Best just to try and forget about it and concentrate on finding Beatticus," said Snowy.

"Agreed," replied Marmalade.

"Agreed," replied Biscuit.

Hours later, they were still walking and Marmalade was feeling exhausted, so they stopped for a rest. Snowy climbed to the top of a tree to see if he could make out the end of the forest before it reached the valley at the foothills of the mountains. "Can you see the end?" asked Marmalade.

"'Fraid not," answered Snowy. "Just forest as far as the eye can see."

Marmalade sighed. "It's going to take forever to get through this forest."

Snowy lowered himself back down onto the ground.

"My feet are killing me," said Biscuit, rubbing his paws.

"I know how you feel," added Marmalade, "and the sun is starting to get low again. Let's just stop here for the night, Snowy, and move on again in the morning. What do you think? It has been quite an exhausting, scary day, and I am knackered."

Snowy looked around. "Fine by me it is, if you are sure?"

"Oh, believe me, I am sure." Marmalade took off her shoes and socks. "That's better," she said, wiggling her toes.

Biscuit curled up beside her on some soft moss while Snowy set up camp and lit a fire. "Are there any Hoppalongers around here?" asked Biscuit.

"No, left them far behind we have," answered Snowy.

"Good," said Biscuit wearily, and he closed his eyes.

Marmalade stretched out on the leaves. "This has been quite a day," she said, staring up through the forest canopy.

"That it has," replied Snowy.

"Can I ask you something, Snowy?"

"Of course."

"If Jedemal had succeeded in his plan to hold me for ransom, would Beatticus have given in to his demands?"

"The truth?"

"The truth," Marmalade said, sitting up.

"No. Beatticus couldn't afford to be held to ransom, even if it was Shatlock's daughter. Otherwise, where would it end?"

"That's what I thought," answered Marmalade, and she closed her eyes as Snowy prepared some supper.

Marmalade wasn't too sure how long she had dozed, but she was woken up by Snowy, who handed her a bowl of soup, which she ate hungrily. Biscuit was still fast asleep so Marmalade didn't disturb him. By this time night had once again fallen, and the only light to be had was the orange-yellow glow of the campfire.

As she ate her supper, Marmalade couldn't help but replay the day's events over and over in her head. Only a few days ago she had come home from school, looking forward to going into town with her friends the following day to try on clothes, look at makeup, go to see a movie, and maybe flirt with some boys from her class over a pizza. She also wondered how her mother was, and if it would have been better if one of her aunts had crossed over instead.

"Feeling better are we?" Snowy asked.

"A lot better, thanks. I was just thinking about how much my life has changed these past few days," she replied. "I got the impression from my aunts that this side of the Portal was like some kind of a Shangri-la, where nothing bad ever happens."

"Well mostly it is," replied Snowy, "but I suppose here is like anywhere else. Some people are never happy with what they have been given, so they decide to take it from somebody else, even if it means using force of arms, and besides, your aunts have never gone any further than the meadows or the river."

Marmalade finished her supper, said goodnight to Snowy, and curled up in her sleeping bag. She still couldn't believe what was happening to her, and she was starting to feel very homesick, but she convinced herself that maybe things would be better in the morning. She certainly hoped so.

Chapter Eighteen

Morning came and Marmalade felt a lot better. She'd had a very peaceful night's sleep, which surprised her, until Snowy confessed that he had put a mild sleeping draught in her soup. Biscuit was also looking a lot brighter and was running around the campsite as if he hadn't a care in the world.

After breakfast, they started off again. They followed a track that wound its way through the trees until it suddenly stopped at a clearing with a small lake in its middle. The three travelers stopped and looked around. The clearing was bathed in sunlight, which cascaded through the trees, making the waters of the lake dance and sparkle. Marmalade thought that it was enchanting. Snowy, though, was not too sure and stopped on the track, sniffing at the air.

"What's wrong?" asked Marmalade.

"Don't know," replied Snowy, "can't say for sure. Something doesn't feel right is all." The three friends suddenly heard a loud roar coming from just beyond the lake where the track re-entered the forest.

"What was that?" asked Biscuit.

Snowy didn't answer at first. He kept staring into the forest, muttering to himself. "Dare say we will find out soon enough," he eventually replied.

No sooner had Snowy finished what he was saying, when a large beast of some kind came lumbering out from the trees. It had the appearance of a wolf only much, much bigger, with tusks that you would see on a wild boar. It stood on the track glaring at them, bellowing and snorting. Great jets of breath came from its nostrils as it exhaled; its eyes were blood red, and its fur was thick and the color of midnight.

"What is that?" asked Marmalade nervously.

"A thousands pounds of bad temper called a Snagtooth," replied Snowy. "But there hasn't been one in this part of the forest for a long time." Marmalade turned to run. "Stay where you are," Snowy said quietly, "and let's see what the beast decides to do."

The Snagtooth stood its ground, glaring at them, and when it bellowed, it seemed to make the very trees shudder. Marmalade suddenly remembered what Snowy had said about his sword. "Don't you think you should call up your sword?" she asked.

"Good idea," said Biscuit.

"No need yet," answered Snowy. "Besides, if it thinks it is needed, it will come." The beast then started to slowly advance towards them.

"Now would be a good time for it to come," said Marmalade anxiously.

"Trust old Snowy. Something tells me this is not as it appears."

The beast then charged, and as it ran, its hooves sounded like thunder. Marmalade screamed, "Please, Snowy, your sword!" Snowy stood quietly as the beast got closer, with his arms folded in front of him, minus a sword, Marmalade noted. The beast ran straight at Snowy, who never flinched or took his eyes off it, and when it was only inches from him, it stopped and gave an almighty roar. Marmalade could see the pinkness of its mouth, with rows of teeth as long as daggers and what appeared to be bits of flesh hanging from them. She could also smell the putrid foulness of its breath, and she shook uncontrollably.

The strangest thing then happened. Snowy raised his right hand and slapped the beast firmly on the end of its nose. The beast seemed quite taken aback by this, stopped its roaring, and stared at Snowy with a surprised look on its face. It then began to transform, and before her very eyes, Marmalade watched the beast change into a fairy.

The fairy was about one foot tall; she had long golden hair and was wearing a brilliant white ankle-length gown. But the thing that Marmalade noticed the most was that she was strikingly attractive, with a white glow that seemed to radiate all around her. She also had a pair of wings on her back that beat as fast as a hummingbird.

The fairy then spoke with a voice that sounded like soft music. "You must be the Snowbeard," she said, smiling at Snowy and rubbing her nose. "My father has often spoken of your courage, and you must be Ms. Tuttle," she said, looking at Marmalade. She then flew down and hovered in front of Biscuit. "And this must be the great Biscuit, who caused such fear in the Narkles." She laughed, stroking Biscuit's head. She hovered in front of the three of them and, bowing slightly, said, "Welcome to the land of the Changlings. My parents have been expecting you. My name is Princess Azeri, and if you follow me, we have prepared a meal in your honor."

"Thank you, your Highness," replied Snowy. "We should be glad of your hospitality."

Azeri flew off, with the three travelers following close behind.

Marmalade was gob smacked. "Would you like to tell me what just happened?" she whispered to Snowy. "And what are Changlings?"

"Changlings," explained Snowy, "are sprites that can transform themselves into any kind of creature. That is why my sword never appeared. It knew that the beast wasn't real and we were in no danger."

"Why didn't you tell ME that? I was terrified!"

"I had to be sure," replied Snowy, grinning.

"And when were you sure?" asked Marmalade.

"When I slapped it on the nose and it didn't bite my head off."

"Oh, I am glad you knew so soon," Marmalade said sarcastically.

Snowy laughed. "I did tell you to trust old Snowy," he said, lifting Biscuit onto his shoulder.

"Yeah. Yeah. So you did."

Azeri led them along a track that wound its way through the forest. Marmalade felt quite excited, considering the events of the past few days. "Who else lives in the forest?"

"It is divided up into four really," Snowy replied. "The Hoppalongers to the south; the Changlings live in the north; over in the east is the land of the Centaurs; and the Tree Dwellers live in the west, but we won't see any of those as we are just heading straight north. Those would be the established peoples, but all other kinds of folk just roam the forest, a bit like nomads."

"Do any normal humans live here?" she asked.

"No, not many, just us witching folk and a few mythical creatures," replied Snowy, laughing.

"Do you know Azeri's parents? 'Cause she said that her dad often spoke of your courage," Biscuit said.

"Aye, I know them. Rulers of the Changlings they are. Her father is called Harlaman, and her mother is called Fezquelir. They have ruled the Changlings for centuries. Well respected they are and well loved by their people, and known throughout the land for their hospitality, so we shall be well looked after."

"A bath and a feather bed would be nice," said Marmalade.

"Oh, I'm sure that could be arranged."

Chapter Nineteen

They walked on for about another hour or so, and Marmalade began to realize that they must be getting close to Azeri's home, as every now and then she caught a glimpse of other Changlings fluttering through the trees. Some would even fly down to stare at them and then dart off back into the forest. "You must excuse my siblings," said Azeri, "but it would appear that their curiosity has got the better of them. When they heard that one had crossed over and would be visiting our lands, they became quite excited."

"That's okay," answered Marmalade. "I would probably be the same. How many brothers and sisters do you have?"

"Too many," Azeri said, "especially when I have to remind them of their manners." She shooed away two very young-looking Changlings that had settled on Marmalade's shoulders. "How many do you have?"

"None. There is just me, my mum, and my aunts."

"And me," added Biscuit.

"Yes and you," said Marmalade. "How could I ever forget you?"

"You must get lonely," said Azeri.

"Sometimes," replied Marmalade, "but I have lots of school friends, so that's okay."

"School, what is school?"

"Mmm, a place we have to go to learn things, when we are children," answered Marmalade.

"Ah. We also have such places," said Azeri. "The Teaching Halls, we call them. My mother and father make us go, but sometimes it is better just to be in the forest and learn from it. The Teaching Halls can be very boring at times, as can the teacher." Azeri laughed.

"Yes. I know exactly what you mean," agreed Marmalade, laughing as well.

A few minutes later, they arrived at the village of the Changlings. The village was made up of dozens of roundhouses of all different sizes, but each one was neatly whitewashed and thatched, with its own garden and flower beds. The largest of the roundhouses stood exactly in the middle, and Marmalade took it that this was the home of the king and his queen. All around the village were paddocks with animals grazing, and fields with different crops growing in them. What looked like hens scratched in the dirt, along with dogs that yelped their objections as they approached. Azeri flew on ahead, and as she reached the largest house, she transformed again into a normal-looking girl of around fourteen years of age.

Before she entered the hut, Azeri asked that the three travelers wait outside. A small crowd had gathered, which started to make Marmalade feel a bit nervous and a bit like an exhibit at a zoo. Snowy seemed to sense her unease. "Don't worry, they are just curious is all," he assured her. "I don't suppose they have ever seen one that has crossed over before." Marmalade looked at the crowd all around her. Some appeared to be very young and were flitting in and out of the houses, while others were a lot older and were whispering in hushed tones to each other. Marmalade tried her best just to ignore them.

Azeri then appeared from inside the house. "My mother and father will see you now," she said.

"Thank you, Your Highness," answered Snowy, bowing low.

"Yes, thank you," repeated Marmalade.

Azeri smiled before telling the rest of the Changlings to go about their business. Marmalade and Biscuit followed Snowy into the hut. The floor of the hut was covered in furs and rushes. It was lit by candles and oil lamps, and intricate tapestries hung all around the walls. A fire glowed in the middle, and its smoke wound its way up through a small opening in the roof. Marmalade could smell a fragrance of herbs and spices, which reminded her of the incense that her mother sometimes used when making spells.

At the far end of the hut sat King Harlaman and Queen Fezquelir. Both were dressed in a very similar fashion to Azeri, with the exception of the circlets they wore on their heads and the chains they wore at their necks.

As he approached, Snowy bowed and knelt on one knee. "Greetings, Your Majesties," he said solemnly.

King Harlaman approached Snowy and raised him to his feet. "Snowy," he said, "you of all people do not need to be so formal." Harlaman then put his arms around Snowy and embraced him fondly. "How long has it been since I saw you, old friend?"

"Too long," answered Snowy, who it must be said was looking slightly embarrassed.

"And how are things in the Meadows?"

"Very quiet, just the way I like it," replied Snowy.

Queen Fezquelir then approached Snowy and kissed him lightly on the cheek. "You are looking well, Snowbeard," she stated, smiling at him.

"As are you, my queen," replied Snowy, blushing.

Harlaman then turned to Marmalade. "I have heard of your plight, Ms. Tuttle, and rest assured I will do whatever I can to assist you," he said kindly.

"Thank you, Your Majesty," replied Marmalade, trying her best to curtsy.

Queen Fezquelir then took Marmalade by the hand and led her over to a large table that was laid out for a feast. "You must be hungry," said the queen, taking Marmalade's rucksack from her and handing it to a maid.

"Starving," replied Marmalade, staring at the delicious food.

"Then eat up. You too, Biscuit," said Fezquelir, smiling.

Marmalade thanked the queen and began to tuck in. The meal consisted of all sorts of wondrous food. There were nuts, fruits, and berries, biscuits and breads, fish, poultry, and sweets. There were jugs of juices and water, along with the now familiar Lambrils' milk. As Marmalade and Biscuit began to eat, they were joined by Snowy and King Harlaman. Queen Fezquelir had left to see to their bathing and sleeping arrangements.

"I am told that you had some trouble with Jedemal," said the king.

"Some," replied Snowy. "Sorry I was of what happened to him, but I had no choice."

"No one likes to hear of the death of a fellow forest dweller," said the king, "but you did what had to be done. Beatticus could not be held to ransom. Who have they declared as their ruler?"

"One who calls himself Gormaleer," answered Snowy as he ate what looked like a chicken leg. "Do you know him?"

"Aye, he is young but wise for his years. He should make a good ruler. Jedemal was a tyrant who tried to stir up old hatreds and animosities. You may have done the Hoppalongers a favor, my friend, in disposing of him."

"Maybe, but that doesn't make what happened sit any easier," answered Snowy, and King Harlaman nodded sympathetically.

"How long have you two known each other?" asked Biscuit.

Harlaman smiled. "Longer than perhaps both of us would care to admit," he answered, drinking some sort of purplish juice. "Long ago, Snowy and I fought together in a war against the Hoppalongers."

"I thought Beatticus settled that," said Marmalade, her mouth full of food.

"He did," answered Snowy, "but not through magic or the like."

"What happened then?" asked Marmalade, completely enthralled.

"Well," said Harlaman, "Beatticus knew that the only way to defeat the Hoppalongers was by force of arms, so he created the Sharron Knights. These were a group of warrior knights who were sworn to Beatticus. Your father, Shatlock, was a commander of Beatticus' most loyal knights. Snowy here was your father's captain, and I, for my sins, was Snowy's master-at-arms. For years we fought the Hoppalongers in a great many battles, until Locklar was captured and brought before the Great Council."

"I take it that they weren't called the Hoppalongers back then?" Marmalade said.

"No, they were known as the Swiftfoot until Beatticus took away their leg."

"What happened to Locklar?"

Snowy lit his pipe. "He was exiled to the frozen waste of the Northern Lands, and there he died, bitter and deranged, some years later."

"The Elders of the Swiftfoot were made to stand before the Council and swear an oath to never again take up arms against any forest dweller, which they did, and there has been peace ever since," added Harlaman.

"Until yesterday," said Marmalade, wiping Lambril juice from her mouth.

"Hopefully that was a one-off," said the king. "Gormaleer knows that it would be foolish to return to the old ways. But come, let us finish our meal and then I can get Azeri to take you around our village."

"I would like that," said Marmalade.

"I think I will pass," said Snowy. "These old bones aren't as young as they used to be." Marmalade and Harlaman laughed, as Biscuit had fallen asleep.

Chapter Twenty

After Marmalade had eaten her fill, Princess Azeri took her on a tour of the village. It seemed to Marmalade like any other normal village, if perhaps a bit medieval. People were going about their normal business and chores, and the youngest Changlings were laughing and playing at chasing each other through the branches of the trees. The one thing that struck Marmalade as decidedly odd, though, was that all the Changlings looked exactly the same, except for the obvious differences in their age. They all had gold-colored hair, and they all wore a white ankle-length robe. Some had the robe tied in the middle by a length of silver twine, whilst others just let their robe hang loose.

Marmalade and Azeri sat down on a bench beside a small fountain. "Tell me about your side of the Portal. What is it like?" asked Azeri.

"A lot different from this," answered Marmalade. "It is noisy, smelly, and crowded. I live in a large town with lots of people who always seem to be in a rush to be going somewhere. There are shops, factories, loads of houses, as well as the movie theatre and the sports complex." Azeri looked puzzled, so Marmalade explained to her what exactly her side of the Portal was like.

"I would like to visit it one day," said Azeri.

"Well, why don't you? Whenever my mum is well, you can come and stay with me."

Azeri smiled. "Thank you, but unfortunately that would not be possible. No one born on this side of the Portal can cross over, except in extreme circumstances, and only with the express permission of Beatticus."

"And I don't suppose visiting me would be considered an extreme circumstance?"

Azeri laughed. "Unfortunately not."

Marmalade and Azeri talked for ages, comparing what their lives were like on each side of the Portal, and as the sun began to set, they made their way back to the Royal Roundhouse. The young Changlings had been brought inside, and the village was becoming deserted as people went home to their own dwellings.

When they reached the roundhouse, Fezquelir was waiting for them. "Come," she said to Marmalade, "I have had a bath prepared for you, as well as some fresh clothes while yours are being cleaned." Marmalade followed Fezquelir through a door into a bathing chamber at the rear of the roundhouse. She undressed and lowered herself into the warm water, which was heaven.

After bathing, she dried herself and put on a robe, the same sort the rest of the Changlings wore. She then joined her hosts in the main living area, feeling completely refreshed. Snowy and Harlaman were talking. Harlaman turned his attention to Marmalade. "In the morning, I will have Azeri and two of her brothers take you to the end of our lands," he stated, "and you can continue your journey from there."

"Thank you again, Your Majesty," replied Marmalade.

"You are welcome. My wife will show you where you can rest."

Marmalade was then taken by the queen to a bedroom, where a bed had been made up for her and which was covered in the softest mosses, ferns, and fur. Marmalade closed her eyes and fell into a deep, restful sleep.

Chapter Twenty-One

When Marmalade woke up the next morning, her clothes were neatly laid out on her bed for her, so she changed and went to find Biscuit and Snowy, who were already up and about, and eating breakfast with the king and queen. Azeri was there also, and she beckoned for Marmalade to come and sit beside her. Whilst they were eating, two male Changlings entered the room. Both looked to be in their late teens and were tall and athletic-looking.

"Ah," said Harlaman to Snowy, "let me introduce you to my eldest sons: Prince Caspian on the right and Prince Ramous."

Snowy stood and bowed his head. "A pleasure to make your acquaintance, Your Majesties."

"Likewise, Snowbeard," replied Caspian. "My father has told us a great deal about you, and this must be young Ms. Tuttle," he continued, beaming a smile at Marmalade.

Marmalade felt a hot flush of embarrassment coming to her cheeks. "Hi," she said, barely audibly.

Caspian then spoke to his father. "Preparations have been made, Father, and we are ready to leave whenever our guests have finished their meal."

Ramous then spoke for the first time. "We would expect to be back by mid afternoon, that's if our little sister can keep up with us," he said, looking at Azeri.

"Don't worry about me," said Azeri. "All you two will see is my tail feathers," she added, laughing.

King Harlaman cleared his throat and addressed his three

children. "This is not a race," he said sternly. "You must take care and remember to avoid the land of the Draak."

"We will, Father, do not worry," answered Caspian.

Snowy then got to his feet and gathered his belongings. "Time to go," he said to Marmalade.

They all made their way out of the roundhouse to a clearing a short distance away. Azeri, Caspian, and Ramous then joined hands in a circle and began to chant some kind of spell. As Marmalade watched, the three Changlings began to transform themselves until eventually they had turned into three enormous eagles, the size of small aircraft.

"Marmalade, you are with me," shouted Azeri. Marmalade climbed onto Azeri's back with Biscuit in her rucksack, while Snowy climbed onto the eagle that was Caspian.

Harlaman approached Snowy. "Take care, my friend, and do not leave it so long before you visit us the next time," he said, shaking his friend's hand.

Fezquelir kissed Marmalade on the cheek and stroked Biscuit's head. "May fate bring you what you seek in life, Marmalade Tuttle, and remember you always are welcome here," she said.

"Thank you for all that you have done," answered Marmalade, "and I promise that I will visit again."

The queen smiled and nodded her head. "I would like that."

Then, with a great screech and a beat of their massive wings, the eagles lifted off into the sky, climbing higher and higher, until the village was just a collection of small dots below them.

Chapter Twenty-Two

The wind rushed through Marmalade's hair as they climbed into the blue sky. Caspian and Snowy led the way with Azeri and Marmalade coming behind. Ramous flew about fifty yards off to Azeri's right and slightly higher. The forest beneath them seemed to go for miles and miles as they flew north towards the mountains, and hopefully to Beatticus Twigg.

"A couple of hours and we should be at the mountains," shouted Azeri. "Are you okay?"

"Yes, I'm fine," shouted Marmalade. "I don't know if I can say the same for Biscuit, though." Azeri laughed.

"Ferrets are not supposed to fly," yelled Biscuit. "If we were, we would have been given feathers and wings instead of fur."

From such a great height, Marmalade could see rivers snaking their way through the forest, ending in what looked like waterfalls that rushed and spilled into great lakes. As she looked west she could see a great ocean, and to the east there appeared to be a desert. She wished that they had time for Azeri to take her on a tour of this side of the Portal, but the great eagles never wavered from their northerly course.

Ramous then flew down to join his sister. "We are coming up on the land of the Draak," he said. "Stay vigilant, little sister, and keep a good lookout."

Azeri nodded her head. "I will," she said.

"What are Draak?" asked Marmalade.

"Flying demons that would think nothing of killing anything

that got too close to them," replied Azeri, "but we are not entering their lands, only passing by, so we will be fine. Besides, Ramous will spot any if they appear, long before they can get close enough to hurt us."

Marmalade felt rather nervous, despite Azeri's reassuring words, and decided that she would keep a lookout as well, even though she didn't know what she was looking out for. Besides, a flying demon would be pretty hard to miss, even for her.

On and on they flew, and Marmalade sensed that a change had come over Azeri. She seemed tenser, and her head was jerking in every direction, watching the sky and the horizon. Suddenly, Marmalade heard Caspian's voice shouting, "A Draak, coming out of the sun! Fly close together and maybe that will deter him." The three eagles were now in a "V" formation, with Caspian in front. Marmalade looked to her right towards the sun and saw a dark shape flying directly towards them, albeit some distance away, breathing fire as it came.

"He is going to attack," shouted Ramous. "I will see if I can draw him off."

Ramous flew directly towards the Draak. The demon breathed more fire as it saw Ramous approach. Its wings seemed to block out the sun, and to Marmalade it looked exactly like a pterodactyl she had seen in her encyclopedia at home, only much larger, larger even than the eagles. Ramous flew straight at the beast, baring his great talons in an effort to fend it off.

The Draak, however, was undeterred, and shrugged off Ramous' attack. Again and again Ramous attacked, trying desperately to prevent the beast from reaching his siblings, but to no avail. Caspian watched as his brother fought and saw that the Draak was gaining the advantage as his brother tired. Caspian then heard Snowy shouting, "Let us help your brother before it is too late." Caspian banked to his right and flew to join his brother. The Draak saw Caspian coming and began to screech its defiance.

"We have to help," shouted Marmalade. "Please, Azeri, we have to help your brothers." Azeri flew after Caspian, who was now engaged in a furious battle with the Draak, along with his brother.

Ramous saw Azeri approach and shouted at her, "No, little sister, stay back! It is too dangerous." As Ramous shouted at Azeri, the Draak saw its chance and whipped its great tail, which smashed into Ramous' side, sending him plummeting towards the ground.

"Ramous!" Azeri shouted as she watched her brother fall. Ramous heard his sister's call and stretched his great wings. His left wing appeared to be damaged, and Marmalade could see blood covering the feathers. Ramous was obviously badly hurt, but flew back to join the others. A deadly aerial ballet then ensued, with all three of the eagles attacking the Draak. As Azeri and Ramous attacked from the front, Caspian attacked from the rear. Suddenly, Marmalade could see that Snowy had his sword in his hand, and with a mighty leap, he landed on the back of the Draak, plunging his sword into its neck again and again.

The Draak screeched and screamed in pain. It twisted its long neck in an attempt to dislodge Snowy as its life's blood flowed from the wounds that Snowy had inflicted. Snowy, realizing that the beast was dying, again leapt into the air and back onto Caspian, who, along with his brother and sister, was exhausted and covered in scars of the battle. It was then that it happened.

The Draak, in a last, desperate act as death took hold, again lashed out with its long tail, causing Azeri to veer sharply to the left. Marmalade lost her grip on her rucksack, and it went spiraling to the valley below with Biscuit inside, along with the Draak. As Marmalade watched, unable to speak, the rucksack opened, and Biscuit came tumbling out. Marmalade could see the terror on his face as he tried desperately to get a foothold in the air, like a character from a cartoon.

"No! Biscuit! No!" she shouted. "Azeri, catch him!" Azeri tried to catch up with the little ferret as he fell, but it was too late. Marmalade buried her face in her hands and wept uncontrollably, so she never saw his little body twist as it hit an outcrop of rock, or heard his cries of pain. Biscuit tumbled down the slope of the valley before coming to a halt not far from the body of the Draak. His eyes were closed, his fur was red, and his chest rose one last time and then fell still. The fight was won, but to Marmalade, the price was unimaginable.

Chapter Twenty-Three

The Changlings landed close to Biscuit's broken body and transformed back. Each one was breathing heavily and covered in wounds, Ramous being the worst, with a large gash that ran the length of his left arm. Marmalade ran over and cradled Biscuit gently in her arms. "This is all my fault," she cried through her tears. "He didn't want to come here, but I made him and now look what has happened. He's dead and it's all my fault."

"I am so sorry, Marmalade," said Azeri gently, with tears in her eyes. "If only I had seen the Draak's tail sooner."

"It is no one's fault but the Draak's," interrupted Ramous, trying to stem the flow of blood from his arm.

Snowy knelt down beside Marmalade. "Give him to me, child," he said softly.

Marmalade reluctantly did as she was told and handed Biscuit's body over to him. "What are you going to do? I don't want him buried here. I want to take him home," she cried through her tears.

Snowy looked at the three Changlings. "Time to invoke Deep Magic. Unless you have any objections," he said.

The Changlings glanced at one another. "No," replied Caspian, "we have no objections, Snowbeard."

"Good. Then I will need your help." Snowy laid Biscuit down on the ground and covered his body with grass. He then reached into his rucksack and took out a small bottle of yellowish liquid. He poured two drops into each of Biscuit's eyes, along with four drops into his mouth. The three Changlings and Snowy knelt in a circle around Biscuit and joined hands. "Erribar, Samminar, Olach, Reiousis," they chanted, softly at first, then louder and louder. As they chanted, a glow emanated from each of them until it completely covered where Biscuit lay. In fact, it seemed to Marmalade that Biscuit himself was glowing.

Suddenly, Marmalade could see stirring in the grass that covered Biscuit's body, and her heart missed a beat. The chanting continued. Each of the Changlings and Snowy had their heads bowed and their eyes shut, as if in deep concentration or prayer. The longer the spell went on, the more Biscuit moved, until he finally sat up through the grass and looked at Marmalade. "Are we there yet?" he asked.

Marmalade was laughing and crying all at the same time. "No, not yet, but soon," she replied through her tears, a beaming smile on her face. The Changlings and Snowy stood up, and the glow disappeared. Marmalade rushed over and lifted Biscuit in her arms, practically hugging the breath out of him. "When we get home I am going to spoil you rotten," she said, kissing Biscuit on the head.

"Biscuit can't go home to your side now, Marmalade," said Snowy, looking at the others.

Marmalade stared at him, disbelieving. "Why not? He was born on my side of the Portal, so he can return there."

"I'm sorry, Marmalade," said Azeri, "but Snowy is right. Biscuit died and was reborn on this side of the Portal, so he belongs here now and cannot return."

"Is that right? Biscuit cannot come home with me?" she asked Snowy imploringly.

"I'm afraid so." Snowy nodded his head.

"But who will look after him?" she said, beginning to cry all over again.

"I will, if he wants me to," replied Snowy, putting his arm around her to console her.

Marmalade looked at her little friend. "Biscuit, what do you want to do?"

"If those are the rules, then those are the rules," replied Biscuit. "Besides, living with Snowy mightn't be that bad, and you can always come and visit. Isn't that right, Snowy?"

Snowy smiled and nodded his head.

"I will miss you, though," said Marmalade, still crying, and hugging Biscuit as hard as she could.

"Me too," replied Biscuit. "Me too."

Caspian then spoke. "We must leave now, my friends, and get Ramous back to our village to have him treated by our healer." Ramous was still bleeding quite badly and appeared to be in quite a bit of pain.

"Thank you for everything that you have done," said Marmalade. "I will never forget you."

Azeri smiled. "And we will never forget you, Marmalade Tuttle," she said. Marmalade hugged Azeri, and Caspian and Ramous kissed her on the cheek.

Caspian took Snowy's hand. "You are truly a brave man, Snowbeard. My father is lucky to have such a warrior as his friend."

"Your father taught me a lot," answered Snowy. "Believe me, it is I who is the lucky one." Caspian nodded. Azeri and Caspian then transformed back into the great eagles, and with Ramous sitting on Caspian's back, they again lifted off into the sky heading south and home.

Chapter Twenty-Four

Marmalade sat on the grass and looked around, feeling drained. They had left the forest behind and were now in a valley at the foothills of the mountains. "I am so glad to be out of that forest," she said.

"Aye, a rough time that was for a couple of days," answered Snowy, "but it should be easier now. We are nearly there."

"How much further?" asked Biscuit.

"Not far now, just up the valley to about halfway up the mountain. We should be there before the darkings descends." Snowy sat down beside Marmalade. "We can rest for a while, and then we must move on," he said gently.

"I know, I know," answered Marmalade. "Just give me a few minutes to get my breath back. It's not every day you fight a flying demon and see your friend raised from the dead." Snowy lit his pipe. "By the way," she added, "that was either a very brave or a very stupid thing, jumping onto the Draak's back like that. You could have been killed, and where would that have left me and Biscuit? Who would he have stayed with then?"

Snowy shrugged his shoulders. "I don't think it was brave or stupid," he said, "but I do think it was necessary. The Changlings were tiring and needed help, so I helped is all. You weren't scared, were you?"

"Not at all," answered Marmalade sarcastically. "I am totally used to seeing one of my friends riding on the back of some dragon or other and plunging a sword into its neck. It happens in our town centre every Saturday night. Doesn't it, Biscuit?"

Snowy and Biscuit started to laugh, and although Marmalade tried her best not to, she began to laugh as well.

After about twenty minutes, Snowy lifted his rucksack and swung it onto his back. Marmalade lifted hers up from where it had fallen and gathered up as much of the contents that she could. She walked down and stood beside the body of the Draak, now lying motionless on the ground.

"Fearsome creature a Draak," said Snowy, standing beside her.

Marmalade nodded. "This side of the Portal is so much different to mine," she said, folding her arms around her.

"It is that," replied Snowy, "but you have some fearsome creatures on your side as well, mind."

"I suppose we do, but we try not to come into contact with them, and we certainly don't have ones that breathe fire."

Biscuit stayed well back from the Draak, even though it was dead, just in case. "Can we just go?" he said, nervously looking at the others.

"I think we should," said Marmalade.

With that, the three travelers left the Draak and headed up the valley towards the mountains.

They had walked for a short distance when they came upon a small river flowing down the valley towards the forest. Snowy nodded to Marmalade. "If we follow this river upstream it should take us straight to Beatticus' cabin."

It was a beautiful day for walking. The sun was shining and the birds were singing, and Marmalade found it hard to believe that such a beautiful land could have creatures in it like the Draak, and said so to Snowy.

"It is just like anywhere else," he explained. "You always have to have opposites to maintain the balance of things. For every good, there is bad; for every light, there is dark. That is just the way it has always been, and most likely the way it will always be."

Marmalade watched as Biscuit ran on slightly ahead exploring as he went. He certainly didn't seem to be suffering any ill side effects from what had happened to him, and Marmalade wondered what he had experienced when he died.

"It's hard to explain," said Biscuit, whenever Marmalade asked. "I felt as if I were floating in a light, and I could hear Snowy and the voices of Azeri and her brothers, and the voices seemed to be pulling me back from where I was floating. Then I was back on the ground and sitting up, and that was about it really."

"Didn't it hurt?"

"Nope, my body felt warm and tingly, but it wasn't sore or anything. Actually it was quite a pleasant experience, but one that I don't want to have to repeat for a long time to come."

They continued to follow the course of the river, and as they rounded one particular bend, Marmalade could make out the shape of a figure some distance away down at the water's edge. As they got closer to the figure, Marmalade was surprised to see what could only be described as something that was a man from the waist up and goat-like from the waist down, sitting on the bank with its hands in the water, muttering to itself.

"Hello!" called Snowy as they approached the creature.

"Ssssh! You will scare away the fish. Sit and be quiet," the creature snapped. It then continued to mutter to itself and feel in the water with its hands. "Gently, gently, Pogel," it was saying, "don't rush. Take your time, easy now. Just tickle its belly like always. Careful, careful, and lift it gently, gently." As the creature was about to lift a fish onto the bank, Biscuit sneezed. The fish jumped out of the creature's hands, back into the water, and swam off as fast as it could. "Aaaaaah!" shouted the creature, splashing in the water after the fish. "What have you done? It's gone, gone. For two days I have been here tickling that fish's belly, and just as I was about to catch it, you ruined it!" The creature glared at Biscuit.

"Sorry," said Biscuit, very apologetically. "I got some grass pollen up my nose, and it made me sneeze."

"Grass! Grass!" replied the creature, who was evidently called Pogel. "Pogel don't get to eat his fish because you get grass up your nose. Oh well, that's alright then, isn't it?" he yelled.

"Whoa! Wait a minute. He didn't mean it, and we are sorry," said Marmalade, coming to Biscuit's defense.

Pogel sat down on the riverbank with his face in his hands. "Two days, two days tickling that fish, and just as I was about to catch it, poof! It's gone. Two days wasted for what, a sneeze from some sort of a talking rat."

"I am not a rat," said Biscuit, rather indignantly. "I am a ferret."

"I don't care what you are," said Pogel. "You lost me my fish."

"You can't be very good at catching fish if you have been trying to catch the same one for two days," said Snowy.

"Yes, well, I am only learning." Pogel looked rather sheepish.

"Oh, and how long have you been learning?" asked Marmalade.

"Seventy-two years," replied Pogel, looking more and more embarrassed. "But I am getting better at it."

"SEVENTY-TWO YEARS!" said Biscuit, laughing. "You would be safer eating something else, mate."

Pogel ignored Biscuit's remark and looked at the three friends. "Just exactly who are you? And why are you here?" Marmalade explained to Pogel who they were and that they were on their way to see Beatticus. "Well, you are going to be disappointed then," said Pogel, "because Beatticus and Shatlock have gone west to sort out some trouble between the Fraylings and the sea merchants. Something to do with taxes that the Fraylings charge for allowing their harbors to be used, although they should be back on the morrow. In the meantime, I suppose you could stay with me."

"Do you know Beatticus?" asked Marmalade.

"Oh, I know him alright," answered Pogel. "I am his, how could you put it, manservant, so to speak."

"Half manservant," Biscuit said with a giggle. Marmalade and Snowy grinned.

"Oh, how very droll," replied Pogel. "I don't think I have ever had anyone say that to me before. Well, if you would like to follow me, I will take you to Beatticus' cabin."

Snowy, Marmalade, and Biscuit followed Pogel as he led the way around a few more bends in the river until they came at last to their destination. At first sight, the home of Beatticus Twigg did not seem to be a very grand affair. It was a large two-storey cabin built entirely of wood, but the wood itself was beautifully carved with all sorts of weird-looking beasts and creatures. From its vantage point high up on the valley, it commanded a magnificent view of the forest and beyond. The windows were all of colored glass and depicted scenes of battles that were fought long ago. In one of the windows, Marmalade swore there was a figure that looked exactly like Snowy, only a lot younger.

"Well, come in, come in," said Pogel, opening the front door. The interior of the cabin was just as ordinary-looking as the outside. There was a living area that had some chairs and a table, and a wood fire burned in the grate. A large pot hung over the fire, and Marmalade caught the aroma of something cooking, which reminded her that she hadn't eaten since breakfast.

"Something smells nice," she said.

"Chicken stew and dumplings," answered Pogel, "and don't worry, there is plenty for everyone if you are hungry."

Off to the right of the living room there were doors that Marmalade took to be bedrooms. In the centre of the cabin was a large spiral staircase that led to the floor above.

"That's where I sleep," said Pogel. "Now, make yourselves at home, and I will serve up supper."

After they had eaten, Pogel listened as Marmalade recounted their adventures and all that had happened.

"Harlaman was right," said Pogel, addressing Snowy, "you have done the Hoppalongers a favor. I know that Beatticus was concerned about Jedemal and his teachings. Gormaleer seems like a good choice, but only time will tell, and I know that he will be interested to hear of your encounter with the Draak."

"Will he be able to cure my mum?" asked Marmalade.

"Oh, he will cure her alright, don't worry about that," Pogel replied, smiling and clearing away the dishes. "I believe Shatlock is your father?"

"So I am told, but I have never met him."

"He is a good man, kind and wise — a rare combination these days." he said as he began to tidy the cabin. "He knows that you are here, and I think he is a little nervous about meeting you. But he talks about you all the time. Takes a keen interest in your schooling and the like. Very proud of you he is, like any man should be of his children." Pogel then sat down beside Snowy, who was smoking his pipe as usual. "Are you the great Snowbeard that was once a captain in the Sharron Knights?"

"That was a very long time ago."

"You do know that is your likeness in the window," said Pogel.

"It must have been a long time ago," said Biscuit. "Snowy looks a lot younger." He laughed.

"Yes, well, as I say, it was a very long time ago and best left in the past where it belongs," replied Snowy.

"Beatticus will be pleased to see such an old friend," said Pogel. Snowy just nodded and continued to smoke his pipe.

As they sat talking, Marmalade heard what sounded like horse hooves outside, and Pogel got up and went to the window. "Seems that Beatticus and Shatlock are home early," he said.

Marmalade's stomach began to turn somersaults; at last she was going to meet her father for the first time. Pogel went outside, and Marmalade could hear voices. A short time later, two men entered the cabin, and what a contrast they were.

One was very tall with long black hair that was plaited and hung down his back. He wore a white shirt, a cloak of deep purple, knee-length riding boots, and black breeches. He was clean shaven and had the bluest eyes that Marmalade had ever seen. The second man was much smaller; in fact, he was only slightly taller than Snowy. He had short-cropped grey hair and a long grey moustache. His face was very wrinkled, and his eyes seemed to sparkle and laugh. He wore a long, ankle-length dark green cloak and sandals, and underneath he wore red trousers and a pale green shirt. Snowy rose as both men entered.

The shorter of the two men approached Snowy, smiling. "Snowy, my dearest friend, how good it is to see you after all these years." he said, clasping Snowy's hands.

"Beatticus," said Snowy, "you are looking well for a wizard of such an advanced age."

"My eyesight isn't what it used to be," replied Beatticus, smiling, "but other than that, I am in perfect health." Beatticus then turned to Marmalade. "Miss Tuttle, I presume. I know why you are here, and rest assured your mother is fine," he said.

"Thank you," replied Marmalade, feeling rather nervous. Snowy and Shatlock embraced like two long lost brothers.

"Marmalade, this is your father," said Snowy.

Marmalade looked at her father and felt the tears welling up in her eyes. "How do you do, sir," she said shyly.

"I would do a lot better if my daughter could give me a hug," replied Shatlock. Marmalade ran to her father and threw herself into his arms. Shatlock hugged her tightly and kissed her cheeks.

"I am so glad that I have found you," said Marmalade as she cried.

"I am too," said her father, tears falling down his own cheeks.

"Let us sit and talk," said Beatticus, feeling his own emotions well up inside him.

Chapter Twenty-Five

Marmalade was the happiest that she had ever been. She had at last found her father, and knew that she would never be miserable ever again. What made things even better, though, was the fact that when her father and Beatticus entered the cabin, she had secretly hoped that her father was the taller of the two men, and so it was. As they talked around the fire, Beatticus sat with Biscuit on his knee, stroking his fur. Marmalade sat cuddled up to her father, feeling very content.

"I must arrange a council with Gormaleer as soon as possible," Beatticus was saying. "If he can prove himself a worthy leader of his people, then who knows, perhaps some day the Hoppalongers could become the Swiftfoot again."

"I think that is what Gormaleer is hoping," replied Snowy.

"So, you have retained the skills that you learned as a Sharron Knight, my friend?" asked Shatlock.

"Some, though it has been many a long year since I have had to use them. So tell me, how did it go with the Fraylings?"

"Fine, fine," replied Beatticus. "They and the sea merchants have reached an understanding without anyone losing face."

Marmalade then spoke. "When will you be able to cure my mother?"

Beatticus looked at her and smiled, his eyes twinkling with the reflection of the fire. "Your mother is already cured."

"But how?" asked Marmalade, feeling very confused. "Don't you have to chant a spell or give her a potion or something?"

"No, my child, as soon as you made the decision to cross over to our side of the Portal to help your mother, she was already on her way to being cured," replied Beatticus.

"I don't understand."

"It is quite simple, Marmalade," said her father, holding her close to him. "There are some things that can be cured or put right by spells or potions, but there are others that cannot. In the case of Morlockins, the only thing that can cure it is a sacrifice made by a loved one. In this case the sacrifice was your coming here and enduring what you did to help your mother. Believe me, what you did is stronger than any spell that Beatticus can conjure up. To put it simply, your coming here and making the journey that you did, facing the dangers that you faced and never once faltering or wanting to go home, cured your mother of her illness. I am very, very proud of you."

"I couldn't have done it without Snowy or Biscuit," replied Marmalade. She ran to Snowy and put her arms around him. "Thank you for everything you did for me," she said. "I don't know how I can ever repay you."

"No need," replied Snowy. "Just make sure that you come and visit from time to time."

"I will, Snowy, I promise." Marmalade suddenly remembered the fact that Biscuit would not be returning home with her.

Beatticus then spoke to her as if he had read her thoughts. "Biscuit can return to your side of the Portal if he wants," said the wizard. "I know what happened with the Draak, and that he was reborn on this side, but I think I could make an exception on this occasion and let him return with you, if that is what he wants. The decision, though, rests with him."

Marmalade knelt down in front of Biscuit, who was still on Beatticus' knee. "It's up to you, Biscuit. If you want to return home, great, but if you want to stay here, that's okay too. Whatever you decide is fine with me," she said.

Biscuit looked up at her with tiny tears in his eyes. "I would love to go with you, but…" he started to say as Marmalade interrupted him.

"But you want to stay here," she said, stroking his head.

Biscuit nodded. "Are you mad at me?"

"Don't be silly. How could I ever be mad at you?"

"It is settled then," said Beatticus softly. "Biscuit will stay with Snowy, if he is agreeable."

Marmalade looked at Snowy. "Make sure that you take good care of him," she said.

"It might be the other way around," laughed her father.

"Could be, could be," said Snowy. "He might have to look after me more than I look after him."

Marmalade felt a twinge of sadness that Biscuit would not be coming home with her, but she knew at least he would be well looked after by Snowy. As she sat in front of the fire, listening to the adults talking, Marmalade felt her eyes starting to close. She was tired, but she was contented. Shatlock lifted his daughter in his arms. "I think it is time you were in bed," he said softly.

Marmalade briefly opened her eyes. "Do I have to go? Just a few more minutes," she said wearily, but before her father had even laid her on top of the bed that Pogel had made up, she was fast asleep.

Chapter Twenty-Six

The next morning Marmalade woke up early. Everyone else was still asleep except for Pogel, who fixing breakfast. "Good morning, miss," he said.

"Morning," said Marmalade, yawning and stretching.

"I hope you slept well."

"Like a baby," she replied.

"Good. I suppose you will be going home this morning?"

It was then that it suddenly dawned on Marmalade that her journey was over, and to her surprise she felt rather sad. "Yes, I suppose I will," she said.

"Looking forward to seeing your aunts and your mother again, I expect," said Pogel.

Marmalade didn't answer, but sat at the table recalling all that had happened in the past few days. Coming home to find her mother with Morlockins and having to pass through the Portal. Meeting up with Snowy. The Narkles, and her journey upriver. Jedemal and the Hoppalongers. Jedemal's fight with Snowy, and his death. Gormaleer. What sort of leader he would make? She wondered if Beatticus would ever restore the Hoppalongers to the way they were. She hoped so. Then there was Azeri and the Changlings. She remembered how terrified she felt before Azeri transformed herself on the track through the forest. Going to their village and meeting King Harlaman and Queen Fezquelir, and the hospitality they showed her.

She smiled and blushed slightly as she remembered Caspian

and Ramous, and she hoped that Ramous' wound had healed after their fight with the Draak. She shuddered as she recalled how Snowy had jumped onto the Draak's back and plunged his sword into its neck, and she remembered the despair she felt as she watched Biscuit fall to the ground, and the joy and elation of his rebirth. But the best thing that happened to her was finding her father and the security she felt when he hugged her. As she sat listening to Pogel talking in the background, not really hearing what he was saying, one thing was certain, Marmalade thought. She would never be the same again.

Her father then appeared. "Good morning, princess," he said. "Did you sleep okay?"

"Yes, thanks," replied Marmalade.

Snowy, Beatticus, and Biscuit then came into the living room, and Pogel served them all breakfast. Although Marmalade was hungry, she didn't really feel like eating. She was nervous about going back home. On this side of the Portal, she was just accepted for what she was — a witch. Nobody quizzed or questioned her, and she didn't have to hide anything from anyone like she did at home. Here they all knew that she was a witch, a descendant from a long line of witches, wizards, and warlocks; and on this side of the Portal, that was the norm. Marmalade was beginning to have doubts about even returning home. If she was completely honest with herself, she felt more at home on this side of the Portal than on hers.

Marmalade decided to take the bull by the horns. "Dad," she said, "I don't want to go home. I want to stay here with you and

Snowy and Beatticus and Biscuit and Pogel. I feel as if I belong here, not at home. I know in my heart that this is where I belong. Please let me stay with you."

Her father put down his glass and looked at Beatticus. "Do not look to me for advice, my friend," said Beatticus. "This is something in which I cannot interfere. It is a matter between you and Marmalade." Snowy and Biscuit went silent.

"I cannot go against your mother's wishes, Marmalade," said Shatlock. "It was her wish that you grow up in the normal world. To have a normal schooling and education, to meet normal friends and do all the things a normal girl of your age would do."

"But that's the point, Dad. I am not normal. I am a witch. I can't tell my friends who or what I really am. I can't have any of them over to stay, or do all the normal things that they do. And what happens when I grow up and meet a boy I like? Am I supposed to tell him what I really am? Chances are you wouldn't see his heels for dust. Then what do I do?"

Snowy cleared his throat. "Far be it from me to interfere, Shatlock, but I think the girl is right. She is a witch and will never be accepted on her side of the Portal. Witches never have been, which is why we created this side. I know that it is not the same now as it used to be in our day, but believe me, the same old prejudices are still there, simmering just beneath the surface. Marmalade will never be able to be herself on her side of the Portal, and you of all people should know that."

"What about your education?" said her father, looking at Marmalade.

"Well, I know a thing or two," answered Beatticus. "It would be a pleasure to tutor Marmalade in both our ways and the ways of her world. I believe that she has great potential, and it would be a pity to waste it."

"Please, Father," implored Marmalade. "Please let me stay."

Shatlock looked at all his friends gathered around the table, and smiled. "It seems that I am outnumbered," he said, "and a Sharron Knight knows when the odds are not in his favor. However, I cannot make this decision without consulting Imelda. If she agrees then I have no objections to your staying here, but you will continue with your schooling, Marmalade. This will not be a holiday. You will have to work hard and study hard if you want to progress to the higher levels."

Marmalade was delighted and ran to hug her father. "I promise that I will study day and night if I have to."

"That is as may be," replied her father, "but we still have to convince your mother."

After breakfast, Marmalade washed and gathered up her things. Her father and Beatticus were waiting for her in the living room. "Are you ready, child?" said Beatticus.

"I just want to say goodbye to Snowy and Biscuit first, just in case Mum says no."

"They are waiting outside," her father said.

Marmalade went outside to where Snowy was standing with Biscuit in his arms, smoking his pipe as usual. "It's not good for you, you know," she said.

"What's not?" said Snowy.

"Smoking that blooming pipe all the time."

"Over six hundred years I have been smoking this pipe," said Snowy, "but I suppose I could try and cut down a bit."

"I don't know where to begin to thank you," said Marmalade, "or show my gratitude for all that you did."

"Your coming back will be gratitude enough, and make sure to give my best to your mother and your aunts."

"Especially Prudence?" teased Marmalade.

"Especially Prudence," said Snowy, smiling.

She then took Biscuit in her arms and kissed and hugged him. "You make sure and behave yourself for Snowy," she said, "and no fights with any catfish." She laughed.

"I don't know what you are worried about," said Biscuit. "Your mother will let you return. I know she will."

"I hope you are right, but just in case she doesn't, I will come and visit you as often as I can," she said, handing Biscuit back to Snowy. Marmalade turned to face Beatticus and her father. "I am ready."

"Then follow me, child," said Beatticus.

Marmalade followed Beatticus and her father for about a mile until they came to a cave that was hidden in the hillside. Her father rolled away the large boulder that concealed the entrance, and they all went inside. Beatticus clicked his fingers, and immediately the cave was lit by thousands of candles, making the walls of the cave shimmer and glow. Marmalade followed the other two to the rear of the cave where there was a small pool, its surface dancing with the reflections of the candles that surrounded it.

"Look into the pool and tell me what you see," said Beatticus.

Marmalade did as she was told. Suddenly, an image began to appear. "I can see my house with my aunts, but no sign of my mother," she replied anxiously.

"Have patience," said her father, "and look again."

Marmalade again looked into the pool, her eyes straining to see into the inky blackness.

"What do you see now?" asked Beatticus.

"My mother, and she is smiling and laughing."

"Good," said Beatticus, "that is how it should be. It is time for you to return to her, along with your father."

"How?" asked Marmalade, still staring at the water.

"It is a leap of faith," said Beatticus. "Just jump into the pool, and you will be home." Marmalade wasn't too sure about what she was being asked to do, and the look on her face must have betrayed her feelings. "Remember, Marmalade, it is a leap of faith."

Marmalade nodded and closed her eyes. Mustering all her courage, she jumped. She braced herself against the expected icy coldness of the water, but instead of splashing into the pool, she was home, standing in the kitchen of her house, with her aunts smiling at her.

"Welcome home, child," they said, embracing her warmly.

"Mum, how is my mum?" asked Marmalade frantically. She then heard her mother's voice behind her.

"I am fine." Marmalade ran to her mother with tears running down her cheeks. "Thank you, my brave girl, for what you have done for me," said her mother, stroking her hair. Shatlock then appeared in the kitchen as well. Her aunts gave a gasp of surprise and bowed their heads.

"Welcome, Lord Shatlock," said Winifred.

"Yes, welcome," repeated Prudence.

Shatlock acknowledged the two aunts, then embraced his wife. "Imelda, looking lovely as ever," he said.

"Why, thank you, Shatlock," said Imelda, "and to what do we owe this unexpected visit?"

Imelda watched as Marmalade and her father exchanged glances. "Shall you tell her or shall I?" said Marmalade.

Imelda smiled. "Let me make it easy for you both." She laughed. "I know why you are here, Shatlock, so don't look so guilty, the pair of you." She then knelt down in front of Marmalade and held her arms. "Are you absolutely sure that this is what you want?" she asked.

Marmalade looked into her mother's face. "Yes, Mum, I am sure."

Imelda nodded her head and stroked her daughter's face. "Then you have my blessing, Marmalade Tuttle." Imelda got to her feet and turned to her husband. "I am depending on you to look after her," she said.

"I will." Shatlock said.

"No more Hoppalongers or Draak." .

"I promise," said Marmalade. "Thank you, Mum. I will visit all the time," she added.

"Just make sure that you do," answered her mum.

The rest of the day Marmalade spent with her parents and her aunts, sorting out what she could take with her. Most of her stuff she had to leave behind, but she didn't care about that. What need would she have for a mobile phone or an iPod where she was going? A new chapter in her life was just beginning, and she was full of excitement. Although this part of her journey had finished, Marmalade knew deep in her heart that there would be many more journeys in the future.

Marmalade said goodbye to her aunts and hugged them both. She then turned to her mother. "Thanks, Mum, for letting me go."

"You're welcome. I suppose I knew deep down in my heart that this day might come, and now it has. Listen to your father and Beatticus, Marmalade, and study hard and you will make a great witch," she said, smiling and hugging her little girl. Although she didn't show it, Imelda's heart was breaking.

"I will," answered Marmalade tearfully, and after embracing her mother, Marmalade and her father stepped back through the Portal, to the new life that lay waiting for her.

The End

Printed in the United Kingdom
by Lightning Source UK Ltd.
135149UK00002B/133-150/P

9 781606 930144